Claudia and the Mystery in the Painting

**Other books by
Ann M. Martin**

Leo the Magnificat
Rachel Parker, Kindergarten Show-off
Eleven Kids, One Summer
Ma and Pa Dracula
Yours Turly, Shirley
Ten Kids, No Pets
Slam Book
Just a Summer Romance
Missing Since Monday
With You and Without You
Me and Katie (the Pest)
Stage Fright
Inside Out
Bummer Summer

Claudia and the Mystery in the Painting

Ann M. Martin

AN
APPLE
PAPERBACK

SCHOLASTIC INC.
New York Toronto London Auckland Sydney

Cover art by Hodges Soileau

ISBN 0-590-05972-6

12 11 10 9 8 7 6 5 4 3 2 1   7 8 9/9 0 1 2/0

Printed in the U.S.A.   40

First Scholastic printing, October 1997

*The author gratefully acknowledges
Vicki Berger Erwin
for her help in
preparing this manuscript.*

Claudia and the Mystery in the Painting

CHAPTER 1

"Claudia! I didn't know you were going to stop by today." My mom stood in the doorway leading to her office behind the main desk at the Stoneybrook Public Library.

I have to admit that the library isn't my favorite place, even though my mom is the head librarian. That's because books and I, Claudia Kishi, don't mix very well — especially school books. Nancy Drew books are a different story. I have them hidden all over my room so I can read one anytime I feel like it. They're hidden because my mom and dad don't consider Nancy Drew "worthwhile reading."

But today I was surrounded by all kinds of worthwhile reading and Mom looked a little surprised as she walked out from behind the desk and gave me a hug. She was wearing a pair of earrings I'd made her: tiny books that really open, hanging from silver wires. The earrings were the only thing that saved her outfit from being totally boring. She wore a plain black skirt and a plain red blouse, and it made her look like — a librarian. There's nothing wrong with that exactly, but I wouldn't be caught dead in anything so ordinary.

Clothes are sort of a hobby for me. I try never to wear the same outfit twice. Today I had on navy blue pants with wide legs, red suspenders decorated with big sunbursts, a white T-shirt, and over it all, a huge red-and-white-checked shirt. My earrings were also bright yellow sunbursts that I made to match the suspenders. My hair was in one long braid hanging down my back, tied with a red-and-white-checked bow. Except for the fact that we're both Japanese-American and have the same color hair and eyes, no one would ever guess that Mom and I are related.

This doesn't mean I love my mom any less. In fact, my entire family is pretty cool, even if they don't look it. My dad's a partner in an investment firm in Stamford, the city nearest to Stoneybrook, Connecticut, where we live. I have one sister, Janine. Mom wouldn't be a bit surprised if *she* turned up at the library. That's because Janine is a full-fledged, authentic genius, with the IQ to prove it. She loves school, books, computers, and all of that stuff. She's a junior at Stoneybrook High School, but she also takes classes at Stoneybrook University in all

2

kinds of things I can't pronounce, let alone spell or understand.

I'm in the seventh grade at Stoneybrook Middle School. I used to be in the eighth grade, but I fell too far behind in my work, so I went back to catch up. It's not that I'm dumb, it's just that school is . . . well, school. It's hard for me to work up a lot of excitement over math and science and spelling when I have all these great ideas in my head. And I do get A's in some classes, such as art.

I love art — painting, sculpting, photography, you name it — and I know I'll use the things I learn in art class. I already do, every day. Mom's and my earrings are just one example. I've taught an art class, I'm an honorary trustee at the Stoneybrook Museum, and I use art all the time when I'm baby-sitting.

I love to baby-sit almost as much as I love art. I belong to this very cool club called the Baby-sitters Club, or BSC, along with some of my friends who like kids as much as I do. But I'll tell you more about that later.

Actually, it was a combination of baby-sitting and art that had brought me to the library. Of course, Mom didn't know that, and she asked (hopefully, I thought), "Are you working on an assignment for school?" When I was in eighth grade and often behind, Mom, Dad, and Janine pitched in to help me with my homework, so you can see why Mom would be excited to think that I might be getting a head start on it. My grandmother, Mimi, used to help too, but she died not long ago. I still miss her.

"I'm trying to find out something about Grandmother Madden, an artist," I said, once again shattering my mom's hopes that some of Janine was rubbing off on me. Although I know my parents are every bit as proud of me as they are of my sister, I think they wish I were a little more like her in some ways. Then again, maybe they wish she were like me in some ways.

"Grandmother Madden?" Mom looked blank. "What's her full name?"

"Grandmother Madden," I repeated. "That's how she signed her artwork and how she's known. She's a folk artist who painted in the primitive style, and she used to live here in Stoneybrook. I'm baby-sitting for her great-grandson tomorrow. His mom inherited her grandmother's house and is getting it ready to sell."

Right in front of my eyes Mom changed into Superlibrarian. I could almost see the outline of a cape trailing behind her. "We can look under Madden, primitive art, folk art, local artists," Mom said as I followed her to the electronic card catalog. Using the electronic card catalog is something I learned to do almost as soon as I learned to read. Mom knew this, but I could tell she wanted to find out about Grandmother Madden too. There are no limits to Superlibrarian's curiosity.

We didn't find anything under Madden, but there was a book called *Primitive Artists of the Twentieth Century* and another with the title *Folk Art*.

Again I followed Mom, to the shelves this time. (She didn't even have to write down the call numbers of the books.) But neither book was there.

Being the head librarian, my mom has her ways of finding out where a book is at all times (thanks to her superpowers and the computer). She clicked a few keys and discovered that both books were checked out. "They're due in at the end of next week. We can put a request in, so you'll be notified when they come back," Mom said, still typing.

"It won't help me for tomorrow, but go ahead," I said. I'd become pretty interested in folk art, and I wanted to find out more about it.

"Wait a minute. Did you say she used to live here in Stoneybrook?" Mom's eyebrows came together and she drummed her fingers on the checkout desk.

I nodded.

"Maybe there's been something about her in

the newspaper." Mom took off again, and I followed again. This time we ended up at the microfilm machines. All the old issues of the *Stoneybrook News* are stored on microfilm.

In no time, Mom had Grandmother Madden's obituary on the screen. She'd been dead for six years. That was weird. Why was her granddaughter just now getting around to selling the house? I knew she hadn't been living in it, because she'd come to town from New York City. Kristy Thomas, our BSC president, said her mom had given Ms. Madden the BSC's phone number.

Besides Rebecca Madden — the woman who had called us for a sitter — one daughter, three other grandchildren, and one great-grandson were listed as survivors. The obituary mentioned that Grandmother Madden had taught art in Stoneybrook, but it didn't say anything about her being an artist.

By the time I finished reading the obituary, Mom had found two more recent articles about Grandmother Madden. They answered all the questions the first article raised but gave me a couple of new ones to think about. They also made me very excited about my new job.

The first article was about folk art in general, but it included a big section on Grandmother Madden:

Folk art, for many years snubbed by the art community for being too simplistic, is finally coming into its own. Artists who once were unable to give their paintings away are now selling their work for undreamed-of prices.

A prime example of this trend is local artist Grandmother Madden. Madden, whose work was savaged by critics in her last show in New York City, withdrew from the art world and spent her final years teaching students the basics of oil painting in a studio in her Stoneybrook home. Recently, when one of the few Madden primitives available was auctioned, it brought in six figures.

There was also a blurry picture of the auctioned painting. It looked like an old-fashioned village with lots of busy people in it. I read on.

Mrs. Madden's work features bright primary and secondary colors and minute detail. Her smallest figures are fully developed, down to freckles on the noses of the children and rings and earrings adorning the adult subjects. Clothes sport lace and buttons, and pets may have tiny cobwebs on their whiskers. Looking inside each door and window rewards the viewer with another scene of what is going on inside the building.

I squinted my eyes and tried to see this in the newspaper picture, but I could barely make out the people and buildings, much less jewelry and windows and whiskers on the animals. I'd have to wait until the next day to see one for real. I asked Mom to make me a copy of the article before she loaded the next one.

FIGHT OVER WILL TURNS OUT TO BE FIGHT OVER NOTHING was the headline:

Rebecca Madden, granddaughter of renowned folk artist Grandmother Madden, prevailed in the five-year court battle that began when her cousins challenged their late grandmother's will.

I compared the dates of the obituary and this article. Grandmother Madden had gone from art teacher to renowned folk artist in six years. I figured that the court case explained why it had taken so long for Rebecca to get around to selling the house.

As it turned out, the battle was over a house rather than the fortune in paintings that the descendants had hoped to find. When Grandmother Madden showed her work in New York City for the last time, sales were disastrous and the reviews brutally negative. After that show, the parties concluded, she destroyed all the paintings still in her possession. No artwork from that show or from any later date can be found. When the cousins learned that they were fighting over a house, they dropped their suit, leaving the entire estate to Rebecca Madden, who is following in her grandmother's artistic footsteps.

"Mom, how could she do it?" I asked, trying to think of something so bad that it would make me destroy my artwork and stop creating new pieces. I couldn't think of a thing. My paintings, my jewelry, my sculpture, my photographs, they are all a part of me. It would hurt too much to wipe them out.

The news that many of Grandmother Madden's paintings had been destroyed quickly raised the value of her existing work. Single paintings owned by each of her grandchildren were estimated to double in value.

"Could you make a copy of this one too?" I asked Mom.

I'd passed by the Madden house many times because it isn't far from my house. It's a big, old house set back from the street, and it has a large yard with lots of trees. Inside there could be lots of places to hide things — including pictures. I'd be spending a lot of time there in the next week or so. Maybe I'd have a chance to look around a little.

"Claudia, there are no paintings," Mom said. "Grandmother Madden destroyed any she'd kept."

I jumped. Mom seemed to be reading my mind. "I couldn't, no matter what anybody said, ever, ever destroy all my artwork," I replied.

"But Mrs. Madden did. It says so in this article." Mom pointed at the paragraph. "Have you been reading Nancy Drew again?"

"Why do you ask that?" I even laughed a little as I put on my most innocent face and reread what the reporter had written. Who were "the parties"? And how had they "concluded" that she'd destroyed the paintings? I wasn't convinced.

"You have a baby-sitting job for this family, not a detective job," Mom reminded me.

Mom knew me well. "Don't worry," I said. "I'm just excited about maybe seeing one of these paintings. Each grandchild has one, right? And the article said that Rebecca Madden is an artist too. We'll have a lot in common."

I tucked the newspaper articles in my backpack. I couldn't wait to show them to my friends in the BSC at our meeting that afternoon.

CHAPTER 2

When I got home from the library, it was almost time for our BSC meeting. We meet every Monday, Wednesday, and Friday, from five-thirty (sharp!) until six. Our meetings always start on time, thanks to President Kristy.

I was hungry, and I knew my friends would be too. I uncovered a few snacks (I have to hide junk food around my room, the same way I hide Nancy Drews). I found a package of M&M's that I'd stuck under my pillow, a couple of Ho-Hos from a box in the closet, and a bag of pretzels that was tucked away in a desk drawer.

As soon as I'd arranged the snacks (meaning, tossed them on the bed) and eaten a handful of M&M's, I dug out the articles on Grandmother Madden that were in my backpack. I wished I could see more details of the painting, but you can imagine how clear a photocopy of a microfilm copy of a newspaper photo comes out. I

11

thought I saw traces of Stoneybrook in the picture, which wouldn't be too far-fetched, since Grandmother Madden had lived here. A picture of my room might be fun to try. I could capture a BSC meeting, with all of us sitting around my room. As I reached out for a pad and pencil, Kristy burst into the room and plopped down in the director's chair.

"What are you drawing?" she asked, twisting to see my pad.

"Nothing yet, but I have this idea. Remember that friend of your mom's, Rebecca Madden? I'm sitting for her son tomorrow, so I went to the library to look up Grandmother Madden, the artist, Rebecca's grandmother. I don't know a lot about her art style. These articles are all I found, but there's some good stuff about missing paintings and fights over her will. And I'd love to be able to see some of the paintings for myself." I handed Kristy the clippings, then quickly sketched her into the picture.

A picture of Kristy sitting still isn't really a picture of her at all. She's always on the move, full of energy and ideas. One thing she doesn't waste any of her energy on is deciding what to wear. I've known her my whole life and she's been dressed in jeans, a turtleneck, and running shoes for most of that time. She's short for an eighth-grader and has brown hair and brown eyes.

Kristy, her mom, her two older brothers, and her younger brother used to live across the street from us. Kristy's dad took off when David Michael, her younger brother, was a baby. When her mom married Watson Brewer not long ago, they all moved into his mansion across town. They can afford to live in a mansion because Watson is a millionaire. And they *need* a big house because in addition to the Thomas kids, Watson has two kids from his first marriage, Karen and Andrew, who live there every other month. Mr. and Mrs. Brewer also adopted a little girl from Vietnam, whom they named Emily Michelle. (She's two and a half now.) Kristy's grandmother, Nannie, moved in after Emily Michelle arrived, to help with the baby. If that's not enough, Kristy's family also has enough pets to stock a small zoo. There's not a whole lot of quiet time at the Thomas/Brewer home.

It was back before there was a Thomas/Brewer household that Kristy came up with the idea for the BSC. One day, when her mom was about to pull her hair out because she'd called all over town and still couldn't find a baby-sitter for David Michael, Kristy thought, what if parents could call one number and reach a bunch of sitters? And now they can. That's one reason Kristy is our president. Then there are all the other good ideas

13

she comes up with, such as keeping a club record book and a club notebook, and creating Kid-Kits. And she makes sure we stick to club business during our meetings too.

If you're wondering what all that stuff is, I'll tell you. The record book contains information about the families we sit for (names, addresses, phone numbers, rates paid), schedules of our baby-sitting jobs, and individual schedules for each of us. The club notebook is more like a journal. We write in it after each of our jobs. Even though I don't like writing in the notebook, I know it keeps us up-to-date. We always know what's going on with our clients, even if we haven't seen some of them for awhile.

Kid-Kits are decorated boxes. Each of us has one, and everybody's is different. In them we put books, stickers, art supplies, toys, games, and lots of other neat stuff. Mine has extra art supplies, naturally. We mainly use the Kid-Kits in special situations — on rainy days, to "welcome" new kids, or when something is going on in the family, such as the arrival of a new baby.

I'm vice-president of the club because we meet in my room, and it's my phone number that parents call to arrange for sitters. I sketched myself on the bed, sketching. I guess making sure we always have snacks helps me keep my job. I drew in some junk food.

Mary Anne Spier arrived next and joined me on the bed. She used to live here on Bradford Court too. She and Kristy are best friends, but they are so different in some ways that I sometimes wonder why they're best friends. Mary Anne is short and has brown hair and brown eyes like Kristy, but her hair has style and her clothes do too (not as much as mine, but a lot more than Kristy's). This wasn't always the case. Mary Anne's mom died when Mary Anne was a baby, so for a long time her family was just her and her dad. He was pretty strict with Mary Anne. He wanted her to wear pigtails and babyish jumpers forever. Finally, Mary Anne convinced him she wasn't a little girl anymore. She cut her hair and started choosing her own clothes. Her dad also let her get a kitten she named Tigger. I drew Mary Anne sitting on the bed, holding Tigger, even though he doesn't come to BSC meetings.

That's not all that changed in the Spier family. Around the same time, Mary Anne and her other best friend, Dawn Schafer, found out that Dawn's mom (who was divorced) and Mr. Spier had dated in high school. They got the two of them back together — and I mean together. They're married now, so Dawn and Mary Anne are sisters as well as best friends. The problem is that Dawn (who had moved to Stoneybrook from California in seventh grade) decided she missed her brother, her dad, and California too much, so she moved back to the West Coast.

Dawn was a BSC member when she lived here, and now she's an honorary member. Plus she started a sitting business of her own, called the We ♥ Kids Club, in California. We all miss Dawn, but Mary Anne misses her the most. Dawn has long blonde hair, blue eyes, and this thing for health food that I've never completely understood. She's also very into the environment. Luckily for us, Dawn comes back to Stoneybrook for visits every chance she gets. Even though Dawn isn't always here, I sketched her into the picture to make it complete.

"This is so sad!" Mary Anne held up the article on Grandmother Madden. I swear she had tears in her eyes. "The family fighting over the will, and this poor artist never knowing that people came to love her paintings."

Did I mention that Mary Anne is not only shy but sensitive? She's also the sweetest person I know *and* the most organized. That's organized with a capital O. That's why she's our secretary and keeps track of the club record book.

I continued to draw the rest of the members as they came in.

I put my best friend, Stacey McGill, on the bed with Mary Anne and me. Stacey likes clothes as much as I do. Unfortunately, the picture I was working on was a pencil sketch, so I couldn't show colors. I drew Stacey's short plaid skirt (and noted that it should be red and black), clunky (black) shoes, ribbed (black) turtleneck, and (red) vest. I made her hair curly, although I couldn't make it blonde, and penciled in her blue eyes. Stacey has a more grown-up look than most of the rest of the club members. That comes, I think, from the fact that she was born and raised in New York City. She moved here in seventh grade, then went back to the city when her dad was transferred there for his job. After her parents divorced, Stacey and her mom returned to Stoneybrook. Stacey often visits her dad, who stayed in the city.

Another thing that makes Stacey seem more grown-up than the rest of us is her diabetes. That's a disease that prevents her body from processing sugar properly. Because of it, Stacey can't eat sugary food and she has to give herself insulin injections every day. It's a lot of responsibility, but Stacey handles it well. She takes good care of herself and stays healthy. She's also the reason I always have pretzels or some other sugar-free snack on hand, in addition to all the junk food.

Stacey's our treasurer, and she loves collecting our dues each Monday. We don't give it up without protests. After all, we work hard for that money! The dues are important, though. We use our funds to pay part of my phone bill; to pay Charlie, Kristy's oldest brother, for driving her and Abby Stevenson to meetings; to restock our Kid-Kit supplies; and, if there's anything left over, for pizza parties. Stacey's good at her job because she's great at math.

Our newest BSC member is Abby Stevenson. It was hard to decide how to draw her in the picture because, like Kristy, Abby is full of energy. She has a crazy sense of humor too. She also has opinions and isn't shy about sharing them, something that has put her at odds with our president at times. I placed her in the middle of the picture because she likes to be the center of attention.

Abby moved to Stoneybrook (in Kristy's neighborhood) from Long Island with her mom and identical twin sister, Anna. Anna and Abby look alike, of course — they both have thick, curly, dark hair and dark eyes — but they're very different. Abby likes sports and Anna likes music; Abby loves action and Anna seeks peace. We invited both of them to join the BSC, but Anna decided she was too busy with her music. She's a serious violinist, and she practices a lot. Anna and Abby's dad died in a car crash when the girls were nine. Abby doesn't like to talk about it. She also has asthma and is allergic to all kinds of stuff. She definitely doesn't let that stop her from doing things, though.

Abby is our alternate officer, which means she fills in for anyone who is absent.

We also have two junior officers, Mallory Pike and Jessica Ramsey. Mal and Jessi are eleven and in the sixth grade at Stoneybrook Middle School. They're junior officers because they can only sit in the daytime, unless it's for their own families.

I drew Mallory reading a book. She has curly, reddish-brown hair and blue eyes, and she wears glasses and braces. She's cute, though she doesn't think so.

Mal is a very experienced baby-sitter. She has *seven* younger brothers and sisters (including triplet brothers). She loves kids and wants to write and illustrate children's books someday.

Although she doesn't usually stand around at our meetings in ballet positions, I put Jessi in my picture balanced on her toes with her arms gracefully poised above her head. She is a gifted ballet dancer. Jessi has huge, dark brown eyes and beautiful dark skin. She has a little sister, Becca, and a baby brother, Squirt (his real name is John Philip, Jr.). She lives with her mom and dad, Becca and Squirt, and their aunt Cecelia. Jessi and Mal are best friends and love horses and books, especially books about horses.

I didn't want to leave out two more V.I.M.s (Very Important Members), but I was running out of space on the paper. I flipped over the page and sketched Shannon Kilbourne and Logan Bruno, our associate members. They weren't at our meeting that day. They don't usually come to meetings, but we call them when we have jobs nobody else can fill.

Shannon lives on Kristy and Abby's street. She's in the eighth grade at Stoneybrook Day School, a private school, and is involved in almost every activity they offer. She's smart and funny, and she loves animals and kids. She has two younger sisters who have given her lots of practice baby-sitting. Shannon has blonde hair that's thick and curly, and blue eyes. I drew her with her dog, a pedigreed Bernese mountain dog named Astrid of Grenville.

In addition to being an associate member and the only guy in our club, Logan is Mary Anne's boyfriend. He's majorly cute, with blue eyes, blondish-brown hair, and a wonderful Southern accent (leftover from his days in Louisville, Kentucky). Sometimes Logan is too busy with sports to baby-sit, so I gave him a football to hold in my sketch.

The phone had rung over and over while I was drawing my "primitive" masterpiece, and

Mary Anne had handed out jobs right and left. That's how the club operates. Whoever is closest to the phone, answers. That person takes the information from the client who's calling and tells him or her that we'll call back. She gives the information to Mary Anne, who checks the record book to see who's available and assigns the job. Then we call the client back to say who the sitter will be.

It was quiet for a moment, so I decided to see what everybody thought about the articles on Grandmother Madden.

"Who has my newspaper clippings?" I asked.

Abby held them up.

"I'm baby-sitting for Rebecca Madden's son — remember when she called? — at her grandmother's house tomorrow," I said. "What do you think of what it says in there?"

"About what?" Abby asked.

"Rebecca Madden is from the city," Stacey observed. We all knew what city she meant.

"It's so sad that the family is fighting," Mary Anne said again.

"About the paintings," I finally said, since they didn't seem to see what had caught my attention.

"The article said she destroyed the ones she still owned," Kristy said.

"I don't believe she destroyed them," I replied.

Everybody leaned in a little closer.

The phone rang and Stacey answered it. "For you, Claud." She held out the receiver.

"Claudia, this is Mrs. O'Neal. I'm a volunteer at the Stoneybrook Museum and I'm in charge of setting up a room for children, to give them a chance to experience different art activities. We're calling it the Kaleidoscope Room. Mr. Snipes said you might be able to help me."

I liked the sound of the Kaleidoscope Room. And of course I love art and working with kids. "Help with what?"

"I've come up with several possible activities, but I want to try them out with some children before we open to the public. Mr. Snipes said you're not only an honorary trustee of the museum but a great professional baby-sitter."

"Well, I baby-sit and I belong to the Baby-sitters Club. I don't know if that makes me great." I had to giggle.

"But you do know some young children you could bring to the museum to try out these activities?"

Mrs. O'Neal sounded tense, as if she expected me to say no. "How many children?" I asked.

"Three or four will be plenty." Now she was starting to sound more hopeful.

"Sure, I could do that."

"Great! That's great!" She was so excited that I wondered how many people had said no — and why they'd said it. "Then I'll see you and your little friends tomorrow morning around ten. Thanks, Claudia. Thanks so much."

"But, but — " I was trying to tell her that tomorrow wouldn't work when the phone clicked. "Mrs. O'Neal? Mrs. O'Neal?" I hung up the receiver and put my head in my hands. "Oh, no. This woman from the museum wants me to bring some of our kids by tomorrow to try out a new art activity room. I said I'd help, but I'm supposed to baby-sit tomorrow."

Mary Anne stepped right in. "Does it have to be you?" she asked.

"I don't think so. She mostly wanted kids to try out the activities. I might be able to take Jimmy, Rebecca Madden's son, but I thought it would be better to get acquainted first."

Mary Anne checked the book. "Abby, you're sitting for Marilyn and Carolyn Arnold. Would you be willing to take them and go in Claud's place? If their mother says it's okay?"

"I bet Corrie Addison would like to go," I put in.

"What would I have to *do*?" Abby asked warily.

"Make sure the kids paint on paper and not on each other," said Kristy.

"That they don't eat the clay," said Stacey.

"Or stick beans up their noses," said Mal.

"Beans?" said Abby.

"Just a joke," Mal said.

Abby's sense of humor seemed to have failed her. She looked pale, as if she were scared of a little art project. I guess I could understand that. I wouldn't exactly be thrilled about coaching a kids' soccer team.

"Can anyone else go with me?" Abby asked.

Mary Anne studied the record book, shaking her head.

"Mrs. O'Neal will be there. She's the one with the ideas. All you have to do is show up with some kids. And we'll even help you round them up. It'll be fun," I assured her.

Famous last words.

CHAPTER 3

A Saturday morning baby-sitting job isn't my favorite thing, but I was so excited about going to a famous artist's house that I didn't mind getting up earlier than usual. I dressed in overalls and a long-sleeved green-and-blue-striped shirt, then put on a green-and-blue-checked cap, pulling my ponytail through the back. I had no idea what kinds of things Jimmy liked to do, but I was ready for anything in this outfit.

I stood at the end of the sidewalk studying the house for a few minutes before I rang the bell. It looked like just the kind of place where an artist should live. There were trees and plants everywhere. I could picture the house in summer when everything was blooming. There would be explosions of color all around the yard. The house was painted a soft gray and the trim was a light pink. It may not sound great, but it looked terrific. A porch with railings painted a darker rose stretched clear across the front, and a driveway ran along the side of the house, past another entrance and a second porch. Ms. Madden had asked me to come to the side door, so I walked along the drive. I looked up at the back of the second story, and I saw every painter's dream. Along the back of the house was a wall of windows. I wasn't sure, but I thought I saw a skylight too. Grandmother Madden's studio had to be up there.

I rang the bell, and a boy with sandy-colored hair and freckles opened it just enough to stick his face out. He didn't say a word.

"Hi, you must be Jimmy. I'm Claudia Kishi."

He still didn't say anything.

"I'm your baby-sitter," I tried again.

He continued to stare at me.

"Can you please tell your mother I'm here?" I asked, thinking he might have been told not to speak to strangers. Or he might be very shy — the quiet type.

"MOM!" he shouted in a voice so loud I was afraid it would crack some of the windows in the studio. Definitely not the quiet type.

"You must be the baby-sitter," a woman said, opening the door and motioning for me to come inside.

"I'm Claudia Kishi," I said again.

"I'm Rebecca Madden and this is my son,

Jimmy Cook." Ms. Madden tried to tuck some strands of brownish hair into the ponytail at the back of her neck. Her denim shirt and jeans were streaked with dust and dirt and she even had some smudges on her face. "Jimmy is seven. He's been a big help to me, but I thought I might accomplish a little more if I could work by myself for awhile. And I knew Jimmy would enjoy having some company." Ms. Madden smiled, but I could tell she had to work at it. In fact, she looked as tired as she was dirty.

"This is a great house," I said. "Maybe Jimmy could give me a tour?"

"He'll be glad to show you around, won't you, Jimbo?"

Jimmy kept his head down as he kicked the hardwood floor with his toe.

"If you have any questions, I'll be upstairs in my grandmother's bedroom," said Ms. Madden, running up a narrow set of wooden stairs that led off the back hallway. She paused halfway up. "Claudia, there have been lots of people trying to talk their way into a preview of the estate sale we're having next Saturday. If you answer the door, don't let anybody inside, okay?"

"Okay." I wouldn't let anybody I didn't know inside anyway. It was one of the rules of the BSC. As Ms. Madden disappeared up the stairs, I felt a little disappointed that we hadn't had time to talk about her grandmother. Maybe we could do that later, when she took a break. Meanwhile, I had something pretty important to do. I squatted down, face-to-face with my new baby-sitting charge. "Hey, Jimmy, could you show me the room upstairs with all the windows? I saw it from outside and it looked cool. What's up there?"

Jimmy gave a little shrug. But he was looking at me out of the corner of his eyes, so I knew he was listening.

"I thought it might be where your great-grandmother painted her pictures," I said.

"Pictures, pictures, pictures. That's all anybody ever talks about around here. There's lots of pictures, all right, but my great-granny didn't paint them. That's what my mom told my dad, anyway."

"May I see them? I like to paint pictures. How about you? Have you ever tried it?" I was testing the waters a little, in case we needed some more kids to try out the new room at the museum. Plus I was curious. It would help me connect with Jimmy if he turned out to be an art lover.

But Jimmy didn't answer my last two questions. All he said was, "Come on." Jimmy stomped up the steps, making a big racket. I followed him quietly.

The upstairs hallway ended at a set of double wooden doors. Jimmy threw them open, and the sunlight poured into the darkened hall. It was so bright it made me blink.

The studio was everything I had thought it would be. Easels were set up around the room and paintings were leaning everywhere. Brushes stuck out of cans and jars and a smell of paint and dust and turpentine hung over it all. I walked around the room, looking at the paintings. Some of them were good and some of them weren't, not even a little. I decided right away they must have been painted by some of Grandmother Madden's students, because the styles and the skill levels varied a lot. The subjects varied too. There were bowls of fruit, vases of flowers, a rocky stream, mountain scenes. . . . And then I saw it.

I picked up the picture and studied it carefully. It was a portrait of a Japanese woman wearing a kimono. The colors were tones of yellow and peach, giving the picture a glow. The woman had shiny dark hair (like mine), almond-shaped eyes (like mine), and a smile that seemed to be hiding a secret. You know the look I mean? The one that shows you know something and want to tell it badly, but you can't. Yet you can't keep it entirely hidden either. That's exactly what her expression looked like to me. Although it wasn't the best work in

29

the room, the way the artist had captured the expression on the subject's face gave it a special quality. (I've worked and worked on doing this and it's not easy. I'm not always satisfied with the way my portraits turn out.) Not only that, the woman in the picture reminded me of Mimi. Looking at the portrait made my chest ache, something that happens every so often when I think about Mimi.

"What do you know that you want to tell the rest of us?" I whispered to the woman in the picture. "I bet you could tell lots of stories about what happened in this studio."

"What did you say?" Jimmy asked me.

Still holding on to the painting, I turned around to look at him. "Nothing. I was admiring this." I held it up.

"It's all gloppy," Jimmy said, then turned back to the easel in front of him and pretended to paint on it with a brush.

The painting did have a texture to it, in the background and in the design of the kimono. I ran my finger gently over the surface of it. It reminded me of a Van Gogh. I had never used texture this way in a painting. It might be fun to try.

Jimmy was still working on his imaginary canvas. "What are you painting?" I asked him.

"A picture of the tree house in the backyard."

"It looks as if you *do* like to paint."

30

He gave me that little shrug again, then said, "A little, I guess, but don't tell my dad."

"Why not?"

"I'm not very good, not like Great-granny or Mom, and anyway, I don't want my dad to get mad at me like he does at Mom whenever she talks about wanting to paint. He says it's silly to spend so much time and money to go to school to learn something she should have learned in kindergarten. I didn't really learn how to paint in kindergarten either." Jimmy laid the brush on the tray in front of the easel.

"You could buy that at our sale for a hundred dollars," he said, pointing at the Japanese portrait.

"I'd like to buy it," I said, realizing that I actually would like to hang it in my room, "but not for a hundred dollars." I wondered how much it would really cost at the sale. I might have to come see if I could afford it. I also wondered exactly what Jimmy meant about his dad's getting mad whenever his mom mentioned painting.

I watched as Jimmy gathered up a collection of paintbrushes and rolled them off the edge of the table one by one. "Do you want to go outside for awhile? Or show me the rest of the house?" I asked him.

Before Jimmy could answer, I heard footsteps on the porch below. I went to the window. A man was standing on the porch steps, looking up. I couldn't tell whether he saw me. He moved out of sight, toward the house.

"There's a man downstairs on the side porch," I said. "We should probably go tell your mom." I remembered what she'd said about people trying to see what was going to be in the sale.

"Maybe it's my dad!" Jimmy straightened up and ran out of the room before I could say anything. I followed him.

"Dad!" Jimmy shouted as he opened the door. Immediately, his shoulders slumped.

I was pretty sure that the man standing in the doorway wasn't Jimmy's dad. He was too young, for one thing. And he was Asian-American. "Hi," he said to me. "You're not . . . Where's Rebecca Madden?" He looked surprised that someone had answered the door.

"No, she's upstairs. Jimmy, please go tell your mother there's someone to see her." I wanted to let the man know that Ms. Madden was at home, but I didn't want to leave him downstairs alone or let him in until Ms. Madden said it was all right.

"That's okay. Don't bother her. I work for the company that's helping her with the sale," he said, turning to leave.

Jimmy trudged up the stairs, looking as sad as he'd looked happy a few minutes earlier.

"Ms. Madden will be here in a minute," I told him firmly. "Please, wait right here until she comes."

"Really, since Rebecca is busy, I'll come back another time," the young man said.

As I watched him walk toward his car, I noticed that he looked up at the second floor a lot. I kept checking over my shoulder while I waited for Ms. Madden to come downstairs. When the man started to get into his car, I went upstairs to find Ms. Madden myself. She might need to talk to him.

Ms. Madden was in a bedroom, lying on the floor, reaching underneath the bed.

"Excuse me," I said from the doorway. She twisted into what had to be an uncomfortable position, her head off the floor and looking over her shoulder.

"Is Jimmy okay?" she asked.

"He's fine," I answered, although her question made me realize I wasn't sure where he was. "But there's a man downstairs who says he works for the estate company. He's leaving, but I thought you might want to talk to him."

Ms. Madden rolled out from under the bed and stood up, brushing dirt off her clothes. "Is it Mr. Ogura?"

"He didn't give his name, but he's Asian-American," I said, immediately feeling silly that I'd been so suspicious. "I didn't know if you'd want him to come inside. You said that there were people trying to get in the house. . . ."

"You did exactly the right thing," Ms. Madden assured me with a smile. "But it's okay to let Mr. Ogura in when he comes by. He's helping me decide how to price some of the pieces that may be valuable."

"Have you seen Jimmy?" I asked. "I sent him up here to find you."

"No, I haven't. Maybe I'll try to catch Mr. Ogura. There are a few things I want to ask him."

After Ms. Madden left, I went into the studio and then into each of the other rooms on the second floor, calling out Jimmy's name. There wasn't a sign of him anyplace.

I ran into Ms. Madden on the front staircase, which was much wider and more open than the stairs leading from the back hallway.

"Did you catch Mr. Ogura?" I asked. I wished I had tried harder to convince him to wait.

Ms. Madden shook her head. "No, and I didn't find Jimmy. But it's not unusual for him to get distracted when you tell him to do something. Go check in the backyard," she said. "There's a tree house near the stream that runs along our property line. You'll probably find him there. That's where he's spent most of his time since we came here."

I ran to the tree house. "Jimmy! Where are you? Jimmy!" I yelled. He didn't answer me, but I heard something like a hiccup, so I climbed up to the tree house.

There he was, in a corner, huddled into a tight little ball. His shoulders were shaking. I crawled to him (I couldn't stand up, because the ceiling was so low) and put my hand on his back. "Hey, what's the matter?" I asked in a soft voice.

"I thought . . . hic . . . I thought it was going to be my daddy. And I miss him. I want to see him. It's been days and days." Jimmy threw himself into my lap and cried louder.

I had no idea if he was going to see his dad anytime soon, so I patted him on the back until he quieted down. It's a good way to comfort just about anybody, especially when you're not sure what to say. Then I took a tissue out of my pocket (I always make sure I have extra tissues when I'm baby-sitting) and wiped his face dry. "Feeling better?" I asked. He nodded. "Let's go tell your mom you're found." Jimmy climbed down and I followed him inside the house.

"Jimmy, I don't want you running off without telling Claudia where you're going," Ms. Madden greeted him. "I have to get this house in shape in one week, and if you frighten your baby-sitter away . . ."

Jimmy looked as if he might start crying again, but then Ms. Madden hugged him. "It's okay," she said. "I just don't know how I'm going to get everything done in time."

"I'll help. We'll help. The Baby-sitters Club, I mean." I jumped in with the offer.

"You will?"

"It'll be fun," I said, starting to worry a little, now that I'd volunteered everybody else. At least I knew I'd enjoy it.

"I can pay," said Ms. Madden. "And you could still help me with Jimmy too. Won't that be fun, Jimbo? To have some big girls around to play with?"

Jimmy didn't say anything. He started kicking the floor with his toe again.

"Jimmy and I are going to New York tomorrow to see his dad."

"We are? Really truly?" Jimmy stood tall, almost smiling.

"Really truly," his mother answered. "And I think his dad is going to come back with us. We won't be home until Monday, late in the day. Could I show you some things that need to be done? That way you could start after school and not have to wait until I return."

I followed her around while she explained what she wanted done in each room. We finally ended up in the studio. "This must be a great place to paint in," I said, trying to work around to the subject of Grandmother Madden.

"It's too bad that my grandmother stopped using it for her studio," Ms. Madden said. "Her students were the ones who painted in here after — "

"Do you really think she destroyed her paintings?" I blurted out. I just could *not* believe that an artist could do that.

"After her last show, when the reviews were so awful, she became terribly discouraged. I do think it's possible to stop believing in yourself. In fact, I've been there." Ms. Madden looked around the room, her eyes sad. "I wish she were around today to see how valuable the paintings she gave each of her grandchildren have become and how much people admire her paintings that are displayed in museums."

"But *all* her paintings? The ones she still had?" I pressed.

"I'm *very* certain there aren't any paintings left here. If there were, my cousins would be here helping me, making sure they didn't miss out on the pot of gold at the end of the rainbow. They were as surprised as I was when Granny left me the house. We had figured she would divide everything equally, even though as a kid I spent more time with her than any of them because I liked to paint as much as she did. When we came to visit, they would run around outside, exploring or climbing up to the tree house, but Granny and I would come up here. I thought it must be like heaven.

"Suzanne and Rob and Julie thought Granny was odd. She didn't dress the way other grand-mothers dressed and she gave us presents she'd made, not bought. Of course, those things are worth a lot of money now. And the paintings that she gave each of us are too. But I wouldn't sell mine for the world." Ms. Madden looked around the studio as if she could still see her grandmother there working. I could guess how she felt because it was the way I felt about Mimi.

"There was a big court battle over the house and the will, but when no Grandmother Mad-den paintings turned up, my cousins decided that I could have the house. And here we are." She spread her arms out. "Lots of paintings, but no Grandmother Maddens."

I followed her gaze around the room, think-ing I might ask her about the Japanese portrait. When I looked at the spot where I'd left it, there was an empty space. The painting was gone!

"Jimmy, what happened to that picture of the Japanese woman — the one you said was all gloppy?" I asked.

"I don't know."

"What are you talking about?" Ms. Madden asked.

"There was a portrait of a woman wearing a kimono, and I put it over there." I pointed. "It's gone."

"Gone? You're sure it's gone?"

I walked around, looking at the paintings, but didn't see the portrait anyplace. It would have been easy to pick out because it was one of the few framed paintings.

"I'd better check the rest of the house." Ms. Madden left. I could hear her moving from room to room. I thought about helping, but since this was the first time I'd been in the house, how would I know if something else were missing?

Jimmy and I still hadn't had much of a chance to play, so I started a game of I Spy. I had just spied something yellow (a plastic banana) when Ms. Madden returned.

"Nothing else seems to be missing," Ms. Madden said. "I'm sure it'll turn up. Maybe you forgot where you put it."

"Maybe," I said. The phone rang, which struck me as odd. I didn't expect phone service in a house that had been shut up for six years. But maybe since Ms. Madden and Jimmy were staying here, they'd had it turned on.

"I'm about ready to finish up for today, Claudia, but let me answer the phone before you go." Ms. Madden hurried out into the hall, followed by Jimmy.

I took one more look around for the Japanese portrait, then went downstairs. Ms. Madden was in the kitchen, twisting the phone cord around her finger as she talked.

"I know I promised I'd get the paintings to you this week, but there's a problem." As I walked into the room, she turned her back to me and said something I couldn't hear, then hung up.

Paintings? What paintings was she talking about? It couldn't be Madden primitives. She'd insisted her grandmother had destroyed all the paintings that she'd still had after her last show.

"Claudia, thanks so much for your help this morning. I enjoyed meeting you, and I know Jimmy enjoyed seeing someone besides me for a change. Let me show you where we keep the key before you leave." Ms. Madden went outside and lifted one of the stones at the edge of the drive. "I keep meaning to have another one made, but I haven't had time yet. I'll leave this one here for you to use Monday, in case we aren't back by the time you arrive."

"I'll see you then," I said.

Jimmy stood behind his mother and waved as I walked away.

So much had happened in the short time I'd been at the house. I couldn't wait until Monday to come back again.

CHAPTER 4

Saturday

When Claudia said that working at the museum would be fun, I took her at her word. I should have listened to that little voice inside me that was saying, "No! No! You don't know anything about art. Stick to soccer." I knew my job would mostly be to make sure the kids painted on paper and not each other (it was), but I didn't count on having to rethink the program for Mrs. O'Neal. At least no one stuck beans up his nose.

Since Mrs. O'Neal had said she was in charge of the Kaleidoscope Room, it hadn't occurred to me that she wouldn't know anything about how to set up projects for kids — fun, creative projects, anyway.

Abby arrived at the museum just as Corrie Addison's and Jamie Newton's parents dropped them off. She would have liked to have had a little time to look around the room without the kids, but it was too late.

"Hi, Abby," Corrie said. "Is Claudia coming?" Corrie's nine years old and she likes art as much as I do. She's good at it too.

"Not today. It's just me," Abby replied.

Corrie looked a little disappointed. "Will any other kids be here?" she asked, twisting her brownish-blonde hair around her finger.

"Marilyn and Carolyn Arnold are supposed to come," Abby said.

Jamie reached up and took Abby's hand. He had a Band-Aid across the back of each of his hands. Jamie is four. He's one of our all-time favorite baby-sitting charges.

"What happened?" Abby asked, touching each Band-Aid lightly. They were decorated with balloons.

"Scratches," he said.

Abby led the kids through the side entrance of the museum. In a cheerful room, a woman wearing a gray silk suit was placing sheets of paper on the table. Her hair was in a perfect French twist and she would have fit in any office in the city, Abby told me later. But she didn't exactly look dressed for art projects.

"Hi, I'm Abby Stevenson from the Babysitters Club. We're here to try out your new room."

The woman turned around quickly. Her hand went to her throat, rubbing the string of pearls she wore around her neck. She smiled stiffly. "How nice of you to come. Abby? I thought Claudia Kishi was coming."

"Claudia had another job this morning, so she asked me to come in her place," said Abby, trying to sound happy about it. She heard Corrie sigh.

"Where *is* Claudee?" Jamie asked.

"She's baby-sitting for someone else," Abby said.

Corrie pulled out a chair and sat down at the table where the woman had set out some paper. Jamie went around to the other side and sat down across from her.

"Paint aprons first, boys and girls," the woman said. She pulled out bright red aprons and dropped one over Corrie's head.

Corrie pulled it down quickly.

"I can do it myself," Jamie said before she could put his on him. He stuck his head through the hole, and twisted the apron around until it was in the right place.

Marilyn Arnold rushed into the room, followed by her twin sister, Carolyn. The twins, who are eight, are identical, like Abby and Anna. And, like Abby and Anna, they're also as different as they are alike. Their mom used to dress them in matching outfits, but lately each girl has developed her own individual style.

Mrs. O'Neal grabbed two more aprons and approached the girls. "Aren't you too cute? Twins," she said. "How does your mother tell you apart?"

"Hi, Marilyn. Hi, Carolyn," Abby greeted them. Actually, it's easy to tell the Arnold twins apart, just by their clothes. They like very different styles. Carolyn was dressed in leggings and a loose top, and Marilyn wore jeans and a T-shirt.

"Where's Claudia?" Carolyn asked. "I thought she'd be here and I wanted her to see this outfit."

"She's baby-sitting," Abby said for the third time.

The girls put on their aprons, then started to wander around the room.

They checked out the tables. On one, some clay was set out, on another, sheets of paper. The others were clear. Easels were set up near the windows, and unopened jars of paint were lined up on the shelves.

"What are we supposed to do with these?" Corrie asked, holding up one of the sheets of paper that Mrs. O'Neal had laid out. The outline of a bear was drawn on one side.

"That's your painting project for today," Mrs. O'Neal said. "Girls, come over here and join us." She rounded up Marilyn and Carolyn, who were sticking their fingers in the clay, and guided them to the paint table.

"Where's the paint?" Jamie asked.

At the mention of paint, Abby's nose started to twitch as if she were going to sneeze. She headed toward the windows and opened each one a little to keep her paint allergy from taking hold.

Mrs. O'Neal put a jar of brown paint in the middle of the table. She had stuck four brushes in it.

"Brown? That's all the paint you have? Brown?" asked Marilyn.

"It's a bear," said Mrs. O'Neal. "And after you're finished, you'll be the first artists to display your work in our special Kaleidoscope Gallery." Mrs. O'Neal walked to the door and pointed at a blank wall in the hall across from the room.

"But what if we want to decorate it?" asked Corrie. Her hands were folded in her lap and she was chewing on her lower lip. "If everyone uses brown paint, they'll all look alike. How will my mom and dad know which one I painted?"

"You'll sign it, of course," said Mrs. O'Neal.

"There are lots of paints here," said Abby, taking down a jar of red, one of purple, another of blue. "How about if we open these?" she asked Mrs. O'Neal. She wondered why Mrs. O'Neal didn't give the kids a sheet of paper and let them make their own bears. And why didn't they use the easels. Abby wanted to say something, but she felt so out of place in the art room that she didn't dare.

Mrs. O'Neal looked at the jar of brown paint already sitting on the table, then at Abby holding the three other jars. "I suppose. I mean, if you're careful not to mix up the colors."

Abby poured paint into some baby food jars she found under the sink and set out more brushes. She sneezed once, but the open windows ventilated the room and she didn't feel too stuffy. Jamie was already painting his bear brown, but the girls waited.

"I think I'll make my bear quilted," said Corrie.

Mrs. O'Neal stood behind her chair and watched, tapping a manicured nail on her front tooth, as Corrie painted a blue square on the bear's stomach.

Carolyn dipped a brush in the purple paint

and splashed a thick line directly down the middle of her bear.

"That's an interesting look for a bear," Mrs. O'Neal said, but Abby could tell that she didn't really approve.

Jamie finished painting his bear and moved to the table where the clay waited. He took a lump and rolled it around on the table, making a long, snakelike cylinder. Mrs. O'Neal followed him, pointing out the molds he could use to make different shapes.

"Mrs. O'Neal?" A voice crackled over a loudspeaker in the room. Carolyn turned toward the sound, and her brush made an arc, carrying purple paint with it. Fortunately, Mrs. O'Neal didn't notice.

"Yes?" Mrs. O'Neal answered, speaking into a mesh-covered intercom in the wall.

"Could you come to the office for a moment? There's someone on the phone who wants to talk to you about the Kaleidoscope Room."

"Abby, can you handle these children for a few minutes?" Mrs. O'Neal asked.

"No problem," Abby replied.

"I'll be right back," Mrs. O'Neal said. When she left the room, Abby thought she looked a bit relieved.

"I got purple paint on my shoes," said Carolyn.

Abby knelt down to check her shoes. She

saw drops of purple paint on the floor and table too. "Let me grab a sponge and we'll wipe it off," she said.

Abby located a new sponge, ran it under some water, and returned to the table. "Carolyn! What are you doing?" While Abby's back was turned, Carolyn had painted purple dots on her white tennis shoes.

"I decided I liked it. I have a shirt at home that has purple stripes, and these shoes will look good with it."

"Let me see." Marilyn moved closer, stepping in a puddle of purple paint.

"Stand still. Stay right where you are," said Abby.

Marilyn backed up, leaving purple prints along the way.

Abby scrubbed with the sponge — first the floor, then the sole of Marilyn's shoe. "Let me rinse this out."

Jamie had returned to the paint table with some small pieces of clay. "Look, Abby. Earrings." He held up small circles of clay decorated with dots of paint. The paint was still wet, so he ended up with paint on his fingers, ears, and neck.

"Cool," said Carolyn.

"Wait a minute. I don't think Mrs. O'Neal wants you to paint the clay. She has these molds . . ." Abby began.

"Boring," said Corrie. "Just like painting this bear. I want a plain sheet of paper so I can paint the picture *I* want to paint."

"I'll see what I can find, but no more painting clay. Okay? At least not right now," Abby amended. She thought painting clay sounded like it might be fun, certainly more fun than sticking clay into molds.

Abby rinsed the sponge and turned back to the table.

Marilyn was in the process of painting purple earrings on Carolyn's ears, while Corrie was painting a tiny blue bird on Jamie's cheek.

"And a necklace. Make me purple pearls like Mrs. O'Neal's white ones," said Carolyn as Marilyn dipped her brush in the paint again.

"Oh, no! Not on your skin," said Abby. "Paint goes on paper, not on people." (She was sure Mrs. O'Neal would approve of that statement.) She grabbed a handful of paper towels and looked toward the door to see if Mrs. O'Neal was anywhere nearby.

"Over to the sinks, all of you," Abby commanded. "Wash the paint off your faces and necks and ears. And wash your hands while you're at it. You can play with the clay when you're all clean."

Jamie grabbed the faucet with a brown hand. The balloons on his Band-Aid, even the Band-

Aid itself, had completely disappeared under the paint.

Abby rubbed soap on her own hands, then took one of Jamie's hands to scrub.

Jamie pulled away. "No, I can do it myself. You help them." He pointed to the three girls at the neighboring sinks.

Abby wet some more paper towels and scrubbed the paint off of Carolyn's ears and neck. Rivers of paint flowed off Marilyn's and Corrie's hands as they held them under the water. Carolyn even had paint in her hair, Abby discovered, washing it out strand by strand.

"How's this?" Corrie asked, holding up her hands.

"Nice," said Abby. "You guys go on and play with some clay for awhile." She turned to inspect Jamie's hands. "No! Jamie, what happened?"

Water was cascading over the edges of the sink — brown water. Jamie's hands were covered in soapsuds tinged with brown. He dipped them into the sink, and more water poured over the edge.

Abby plunged her hand into the dirty water. A lump of clay rested on the bottom of the sink, acting as a drain plug.

"There wasn't a plug, so I made one out of clay," Jamie explained proudly. He finished

51

rinsing his hands under the clear running water, then shook them dry.

Using more paper towels, Abby wiped the water off the floor.

"What happened here?" Mrs. O'Neal's voice made Abby look up quickly. Mrs. O'Neal had a tight grip on her pearls as she surveyed the room. "My room. My nice, clean room!"

"It's okay. We're just cleaning up," said Abby with a weary smile. She looked down and saw streaks of purple and brown paint on her jeans. "Art projects are messy, Mrs. O'Neal, and you can't expect kids to learn how to use paint and clay without getting a little bit messy." Abby's reluctance to speak up had disappeared along with the dirty water.

Carolyn chose that moment to show the clay beads she'd made into a necklace to Mrs. O'Neal. She brushed against her skirt.

Mrs. O'Neal looked down, her eyes widened, and she jumped back. "Stop! Stop right where you are. This isn't going to work. Paint on the floor! Paint on your hands! Paint on my skirt! This isn't art. It's chaos. I thought I'd invited young artists to work in here, not hooligans."

Carolyn looked toward Abby.

Abby hurried to Carolyn's side and gave her a hug. The rest of the children remained frozen in their chairs.

With her arm around Carolyn, Abby said, "Mrs. O'Neal, this room *could* work. Maybe if you gave the kids blank paper and paints and let them make whatever they wanted instead of expecting them to make what you want them to, they wouldn't have to paint on themselves. Give us another chance. Let me come back with some help, and we'll show you how much fun it can be."

"Chaos. It looks like chaos in here. What was I thinking?" Mrs. O'Neal murmured.

Corrie was now standing next to Abby. "I'll come back if I can paint what I want," she said. "I want to hang one of my pictures in the museum."

"Me too," said Marilyn.

Jamie continued to roll the clay into thinner and thinner strips. "I'd like to come back and work with the clay some more," he said.

"Mrs. O'Neal?" Abby said.

"You may try again, if you want, but I need to think about some guidelines that will prevent another fiasco like today's."

Abby closed her eyes. "We'll be thinking about it too," she said, counting on the BSC to come through.

CHAPTER 5

I was studying rocks in the Maddens' side yard when the Junk Bucket, Charlie Thomas's car, pulled up.

"Hey, Claud, planning a rock sculpture?" Charlie asked as Kristy climbed out of the car.

He wouldn't have heard my answer even if I'd given him one, because Kristy slammed the car door hard enough to make the Junk Bucket shimmy. Charlie left us in his dust.

Actually, I was already in the dust, kneeling by the rocks. I was trying to remember which rock the key was under. I had thought it was the one shaped like a soup tureen covered with ripples like ocean waves, but that one was firmly stuck in the ground. I tried to remove a second one, shaped more like a boat with tiny mountains all over it, and it came up easily. The key was there, just as Ms. Madden had promised before she and Jimmy had left for New York City. I was setting the rock back when a red Mercedes pulled up beside us.

I stuck the key in my pocket and nudged the stone back into place, standing on it for good measure.

"Is Rebecca here?" The man in the car was the one who had come by the house on Saturday morning. He looked up at the studio windows.

"Not yet," I replied as pleasantly as I could. I had this feeling he was going to —

"No problem. I'll go on in and take a look at some things she wanted another appraisal on," he said, shutting the car door.

"Could you come back later? When Ms. Madden is here?" said Kristy.

"It's fine, girls. I'm just doing my job," the man said. As I watched him walk toward the porch I tried to remember the name Ms. Madden had mentioned. "My company has been taking care of this house for years."

Then why didn't he have a key? I wondered.

Kristy looked at me as if she were waiting for me to stop him. It was a look that said, "Is this guy for real?"

I nodded to let Kristy know it was okay for him to go inside, then glanced over my shoulder at his car. It was fire-engine red with a black top. Very cool. The seats were black too — black leather. I took a second look. There was a book on the passenger's seat. On the front cover was a picture I recognized from my research on primitive art. It was one of the books I was waiting for. I couldn't see the picture completely because an airline ticket folder was lying on top of it. The name "Ogura" was printed on the folder. Right, that's what Ms. Madden had said.

"Mr. Ogura?" I called after him.

He motioned for me to follow him on to the porch, but I wanted to see the book.

"Do you know this guy?" Kristy asked.

"He was here the other day too. And Ms. Madden did say he was helping her with the sale."

"Then I guess it's — "

"The phone is ringing! Maybe it's Rebecca and you can get her okay to let me in," he called. "Tell her it's Mr. Ogura." He was holding the screen door open and tapping his foot.

I ran to the porch and fumbled with the key. The door finally opened, and I almost fell into the hall. Kristy and Mr. Ogura were right behind me. I hurried into the kitchen and yanked the phone out of the cradle. "Hello!"

"Hello," a woman's voice answered me. "Is Mr. Ogura there by any chance?"

I turned slowly, holding the phone out. "Mr. Ogura, it's for you."

He was already on his way upstairs. He

turned, a puzzled expression on his face. "Who is it?"

I shrugged. "A woman."

Mr. Ogura jerked the phone away, then stepped around me and turned his back to us. "Hello," he said in a low, deep voice. "Hello," he said a little louder. He turned around and glared at me. "You cut off whoever was calling and didn't even get a name. I'll call my office. If it isn't my secretary, then perhaps she'll know who was trying to reach me."

Again, he huddled close to the phone, as if he were going to deliver some important confidential information, and punched the buttons.

"Come on, I'll show you the studio," I said to Kristy. I was sure Mr. Ogura wasn't going to say anything I cared about overhearing, no matter how important he thought he was. "It's the greatest room — lots of light and easels set up all over the place." We went up the back stairs and again I was surprised when I pulled open the doors to the studio and light flooded the hall.

"Cool," said Kristy, taking a step inside and looking at the room from the entrance. "She painted a lot of pictures!"

"None of these are by Grandmother Madden," I said. "They were done by her students." I heard a car start and looked out to see Mr. Ogura driving away. "He's gone. I guess that call was important."

"Where should we start?" Kristy asked.

Before I could tell her, the doorbell rang.

We went down the front staircase this time. I looked through the oval window in the front door and was glad to see Ms. Madden standing on the porch. Of course, I had the only key to the house in my pocket. I opened the door.

"Hi. Is this where the estate sale is?" the woman asked.

It wasn't Ms. Madden after all. But her hair was the same color, and she was about the same size.

"The sale is Saturday," I said.

"I've driven over a hundred miles," the woman explained in a soft voice, "because Grandmother Madden is one of my all-time favorite artists. I'd love to have a peek at where she lived. May I?" She smiled nicely and took a step forward.

I moved to block the doorway, and Kristy stood close to my shoulder. "Sorry," I said, "but no one is allowed in until Saturday." I returned the woman's smile. I knew how it felt to admire an artist and want to have a glimpse of how she lived.

Another car turned into the driveway, and I recognized Ms. Madden and Jimmy for sure this time. "There's the owner of the house," I said to the woman. "You could ask her if you want. Wait a minute and I'll ask her if she can come talk to you." I closed the door, feeling a little rude leaving her there, and met Ms. Madden at the side door.

Jimmy almost knocked Kristy and me over as he ran by us and up the steps without even a "Hi."

"Jimmy! Come back here," Ms. Madden called after him.

"What's wrong?" Kristy asked.

"Kristy! How nice to see you again," Ms. Madden greeted her before answering her question. "Jimmy didn't want to come back with me," she said. "He's getting so tired of being here while I prepare for the sale. I'd hoped his dad would be able to come back with us and watch Jimmy, but he had to work . . . again. At least he'll be here this evening." Ms. Madden tossed her purse on the kitchen counter. "Is there someone waiting on the front porch? For me? I have some stuff to bring in from the car. . . ."

"She wants to come in and have a look around," I said. "I'll unload the stuff from your car if you want to go talk to her."

"I'll talk to her *after* I unload the car." Ms. Madden pushed her hair out of her face.

I followed her outside to the driveway and waited while she opened the trunk of her car. Ms. Madden took out a box of cleaning supplies, and I started to pick up a flat package wrapped in brown paper. From the size and shape, I guessed that it was a painting. My heart did a little flip-flop. Maybe she'd brought her grandmother's painting for me to see.

"Leave that where it is!" Ms. Madden said sharply, and I pulled my hand away. "I don't need it yet," she said a little more pleasantly. "You could close the trunk for me." She smiled, but it wasn't much of a smile. She could have been just stretching her lips.

"I have an idea." Kristy met us at the door with this unsurprising statement. (She always has an idea.) "I could call someone to come over and play with Jimmy. Maybe Mal could bring one of her brothers."

"Jimmy would love that," Ms. Madden said, "and I'd love for Jimmy to be happy here for a change." This time her smile looked a little more like she meant it.

Kristy picked up the phone, then put it back. "It's making a weird sound," she said, putting it up to her ear again, then punching the disconnect a few times. "It sounds as if it was off the hook."

"Maybe Mr. Ogura didn't hang it up all the way," I said.

"Mr. Ogura was here again?" Ms. Madden asked.

"He wanted to have a look at something.

You told me it was all right to let him in," I reminded her.

"Isn't he the nicest man?" Ms. Madden said. "He's been such a help with the house and the sale."

I hadn't seen this side of Mr. Ogura yet, but if Ms. Madden said it was so . . . I remembered the woman we'd left standing outside. "Ms. Madden, that woman at the front door?"

"Okay, sure." She followed me down the hall.

"This is Ms. Madden," I said as I opened the door. But no one was there. "I guess she got tired of waiting."

"Some people." Ms. Madden shook her head. "I don't understand why they think they're entitled to see things before anyone else does."

Jimmy joined us in the front hall, standing close to his mom.

"Stacey! Mary Anne! Come on in here," I called to my friends. I'd spotted them standing on the sidewalk, looking at the house as if they weren't sure it was the right place.

"So much help!" said Ms. Madden. "We may have things ready for this sale after all."

"Great house," said Mary Anne.

"This is Stacey and Mary Anne," I said, introducing my friends. "This is Ms. Madden.

Her grandmother lived here. And this," I pulled Jimmy out from behind his mother, "is Jimmy."

"Nice to meet you all," Ms. Madden said.

"I called Mal to see if she could bring one of her brothers over, but they're busy," said Kristy.

"Maybe someone could come over tomorrow," said Ms. Madden. "Anyway, thanks so much for stopping by to help. Let's see. Stacey, you can go upstairs and start on the closets. Mr. Ogura tells me that my grandmother's vintage clothing might sell for a good price."

How did Ms. Madden know that Stacey would love to go through closets and sort clothes? She must have been talking to Kristy's mother.

"Mary Anne, could you go into the library and try to sort the books by category? There are books all over the place, and I'd like all of them to go on the shelves. Mr. Ogura is going to have a look through them to see if there's anything rare, but otherwise we'll sell most of them for a dollar a book. And, Kristy, I need you to take the covers off the furniture in the living room and library. Okay?"

I pointed everyone toward the places they'd been assigned. "Jimmy, how about if we go up to the studio?" I asked.

"I guess," he mumbled.

"You guys!" I exclaimed suddenly. My friends turned around. "There's a painting I saw the first day I was here. It's a portrait of a Japanese woman with lots of yellow and peach in it. If you see it anyplace, will you let me know?"

Before Jimmy and I even reached the studio, Stacey pulled us into a bedroom to look at some hats she'd found on a shelf. There was a small black velvet one, some large straw ones, several with net veils, and some wide-brimmed men's hats.

Stacey tried on a small red hat with a sequined veil, and I arranged a black velvet beret on Jimmy so it hung to one side of his head.

To me, he looked like a Parisian artist. But he took one look in the mirror and pulled it off. "You try it on. I think I like this one better," Jimmy said, plopping a black felt fedora on his head. His eyes and ears disappeared as the brim came to rest on the bridge of his nose.

Jimmy laughed with us when he saw his reflection.

"Claudia! Come here a minute," Mary Anne called from downstairs. "I found something you might be interested in."

At this rate, I wasn't going to accomplish much. "You want to go with me or stay here with Stacey?" I asked Jimmy. As an answer he plopped down on the bed.

I ran downstairs.

"Look!" Mary Anne held out a book, but it wasn't a regular book. I recognized it immediately because I have one like it in my room. It looked like a book on the outside, but the cover opened to a hollow middle.

I reached inside and pulled out a newspaper clipping, a small, glossy catalog, and a piece of folded paper with a list typed on it.

Kristy joined us, pulling a dust cover off a chair as she walked past it.

"What is it?" she asked, trying to see over my shoulder.

I read aloud the headline on the clipping.

MADDEN SHOW A HOBBY SHOWCASE

A Connecticut artist with the cutesy signature Grandmother Madden demonstrates that it's possible for anyone to have a show in New York City today. Her collection of paintings displays the skill of an amateur and has all the life of a stagnant pond. Stick figures inhabit scenes that no art lover would recognize.

How that must have stung! I couldn't even read the rest. To put so much work into your art, then have someone dismiss it so cruelly. I was beginning to understand why Grandmother Madden had lost her confidence.

"And this is her catalog for that show." I paged through it.

"Stoneybrook," said Kristy, pointing at the picture of a painting that showed some of the landmarks of our town — the lighthouse, Ambrose's Sawmill, and even the Stoneybrook Public Library.

"I don't think they're boring at all," said Mary Anne. "That reviewer didn't have to be so mean about her paintings."

"The paintings aren't very big, are they? And they're all the same shape," said Kristy.

"Some artists paint that way. It becomes part of their style," I explained. "Like the colors they work with and their subjects. See how she used bright colors in every picture?" I thought the paintings were great. The people looked as if they were moving through the scenes, and each one of them was painted in so much detail. The women wore lace collars. The men had cuff links. Streaks of dirt were on the children's clothes and faces. I didn't know if I could paint so much in so small a space. There wasn't one thing the reviewer said about Grandmother Madden that I agreed with.

"What do you have there?" Ms. Madden bustled into the room.

"Mary Anne found this when she was sorting the books," I said, handing over the catalog and review. I still hadn't had a chance to look at the list.

"My grandmother's last show." Ms. Madden

gazed at each painting. "And look at this."

She'd opened the catalog to the last page, which showed a group of paintings as they'd been hung. "Granny's small paintings often fit together into a larger work. They each stand alone, but they can be combined side by side, up and down, or in a square."

I was fascinated. The amount of planning that must have gone into these paintings!

"She had a special way of fitting them together if anyone wanted to buy more than one. In fact, the four paintings she gave to me and my cousins form one large painting. They'll never be displayed together the way things are going between us, but if you ever saw it as a whole . . ." Ms. Madden sighed.

"Here's a list of paintings," I said, handing her the typed sheet.

Ms. Madden took it, then nodded. "This includes everything that she'd done up to the time of the show. Grandmother was very hard on herself and worked on each painting for months, sometimes years. You can tell by the details how much time she put into each of them. Let's see." Ms. Madden moved her finger down the list. "Twenty-two, that sounds about right. She gave my dad and my aunt each a painting, one to each one of her grandchildren, and she sold two in spite of this." She held up the review. "And there are maybe three others that she sold before this show. I think they're all in museums now. There's one at the Stoneybrook Museum, in fact, but I haven't had a chance to go see it yet."

Ms. Madden looked over the list again. "Twenty-two paintings, then she never painted again — and there are only half of these left."

I took the catalog and looked at each painting again, trying to memorize them so I'd recognize one if I saw it.

"What should we do with these?" Mary Anne asked, holding up the newspaper clipping, then pointing at the catalog I was studying and the list Ms. Madden held. As I said, Mary Anne is super-organized.

"Leave them on the library table and I'll look at them later," said Ms. Madden. "They may be the only record of some of the paintings."

I still couldn't accept that Grandmother Madden had destroyed her paintings. I knew the BSC had a big job ahead of us, helping Ms. Madden get ready for the sale. We couldn't tear the house apart, hunting for paintings. Besides, the Madden cousins had probably already done that. But I couldn't shake the feeling that the missing paintings still existed — and that if we kept our eyes open as we worked, we might find a clue to their whereabouts.

CHAPTER 6

"You brought a different crew with you today," Ms. Madden said when she answered the door Tuesday afternoon and four of us trooped in.

"This is Nicky. He's come to play with Jimmy." I put my hand on Nicky's shoulder. "He's Mal's brother. This is Mallory and Jessi," I said, continuing my introductions. "This is Ms. Madden and Jimmy."

"Thanks so much for helping out," said Ms. Madden. "Claudia, you know what needs to be done, so I wonder if you'd put everyone to work. I have to run some errands, but I'll be back as soon as possible. Jimmy, listen to Claudia," she said, and she was gone.

"Jimmy, do you want to show Nicky around the house?" I asked. Jimmy was sitting on the bottom step of the back staircase, his chin resting in his hands, staring at the floor.

He shrugged.

Mallory knelt beside him. "I saw something down at the end of the yard. I'm not sure what it was, but it looked like — "

"You want to see my tree house?" Jimmy asked her. "It's not my tree house for always, but it's mine for now."

"Sure," said Mallory. "Can Nicky come too?"

Jimmy nodded.

"I guess I'll go to the tree house," said Mallory, taking charge of the baby-sitting duties for that day and freeing me to go back to the studio to work.

"Jessi, how about going in the library and sorting through the books?" I said. "Ms. Madden wants them all on the shelves, by subject, if you can. I think Mary Anne was doing general categories like fiction, history, art books. If you have any questions, I'll be upstairs." And that's where I headed. I knew that Jessi would be happy working with books for as long as it took.

I was halfway into the room, heading for a pile of paintings leaning against the wall, before I noticed the man in the studio. "Whoa!" I said, then felt a little stupid and scared all at once. "What are you doing here?"

"I'm helping Rebecca," he said gruffly. "I'm her husband."

The man was youngish, with wavy, sandy-colored hair. I thought he'd be cute if he didn't look so grumpy.

"I'm Claudia, from the Baby-Sitters Club. I'm helping too," I said. I wanted so much to look through the paintings, but Ms. Madden's husband stood between me and them. I wasn't sure what I should do.

"I think I can handle things in here," he said. "You go help out downstairs."

"Sure," I replied. I glanced over my shoulder a couple of times on my way to the front stairs. He seemed to forget about me pretty quickly. He was looking through the stacks of paintings in the studio, one by one, very slowly.

A piece of paper rose into the air at my feet, then settled slowly on the step in front of me. I leaned over to pick it up and recognized it immediately. It was the list that we'd found in the fake book the day before. At least, it was a copy of the list. On this one check marks had been made by the names of some of the paintings and lines had been drawn through several others. I decided to compare it to the paintings listed in the catalog for Grandmother Madden's last show to see if I could figure out what the checks and lines meant.

I poked my head in the library doorway. "Hey, Jessi, have you seen a catalog — it looks sort of like a magazine — of an art exhibit? Mary Anne found it in here yesterday. I thought she left it on the table, but maybe Ms. Madden moved it."

Jessi put down the book she'd been glancing through and looked around the room. "I haven't seen it anyplace, but I haven't really looked for anything like that either."

I pulled the fake book off the shelf and opened it. It was empty. I checked shelves, tables, and even under chairs, but the catalog was nowhere to be found.

"What was in the catalog?" Jessi asked.

"Lists and illustrations of the paintings in Grandmother Madden's last show," I replied. "I wanted to look at it again."

"If I see it, I'll call you," Jessi said and turned back to the bookshelves.

I knew I should start working, but instead I wandered through each room of the house, looking for . . . I don't know what. I ended up in the kitchen. Kristy had started sorting dishes into boxes the day before. I pulled a few plates out of the cabinet and stacked them beside matching cups.

"Mom! Dad! Look what we found!" Jimmy burst into the house, followed by Nicky and Mal. Mal was holding a large golden-colored cat. "Where's my mom?" Jimmy asked.

"She went to run some errands," I said.

Jimmy called up the stairs. "Dad! Come here a minute. I have a surprise for you."

Jimmy was so excited. For the first time since I'd met him, he looked totally happy. He had on a smile that wouldn't stop as he knelt by Mal and the cat, stroking the cat's soft fur.

Before I could say anything, Jimmy's dad came halfway down the stairs and stopped.

"Look, Dad, a cat. Can we keep it? Please?"

"It was in the tree house," Nicky said.

"It has an injured paw," Mal said. "Somehow it climbed up into the tree house, but it couldn't jump down because of its paw. Look." Mal set the cat down on the floor and it limped toward Jimmy, then rubbed against his leg.

"It likes me. See, it really does." Jimmy leaned down and kissed the cat on the top of its head.

"The cat has a collar," I said, giving it a pat. It was purring loudly as Nicky and Jimmy stroked it.

"That means it may belong to someone else," Jimmy's dad said. He scooped up the cat and looked at its paw. "There's a nasty cut here. That's why it's limping." He gently set the cat down again.

"Look. There's a name," said Mal, examining the collar. Jessi had joined us, and everyone was grouped tightly around the cat, who seemed to love the attention.

"Goldie," said Jimmy. "Its name is Goldie. I bet she's a girl."

I heard a gasp from the doorway.

"A cat, Mom, we found a cat!" said Jimmy.

The rest of us moved aside, so Jimmy could show his mom the injured cat.

Ms. Madden turned pale and leaned against the doorjamb. "Goldie?" she said.

"That's her name," said Jimmy's dad. "It's here on her collar."

"It can't be," said Ms. Madden.

"Why?" Jimmy's dad asked.

"Granny had a cat. She looked exactly like that one, and her name was Goldie. In fact, Granny had several cats that looked like that, all named Goldie. When one died, she got another. The one she had when she died went home with my aunt in Arizona. But for a minute I thought . . ." Ms. Madden shook her head.

"Can we keep this one, Mom? Please?" Jimmy asked.

"Son, she has a collar, so she must belong to someone," his dad said.

"The poor little thing is hurt. I'll bet she's hungry too," said Ms. Madden. "We'll take care of you, little one." She reached out and scratched the cat's head. "We'll take you to the vet and have that paw fixed up." The cat stretched out on the floor, still purring.

"There's an animal emergency clinic not too far away," I said. "And they might even know who the cat belongs to. People call them about lost pets."

"I want Goldie to stay with us," Jimmy said.

"She can stay here until we find her owner," said Jimmy's dad. "Come on, let's get her to the vet."

"You're my cat, aren't you, Goldie? You like me. I know you do," Jimmy whispered, not very softly, into her ear.

"It was silly of me to think for even a moment that this could be Granny's cat," Ms. Madden said. "This is a pretty common color for a cat and probably a common name too. I'll leave it to you girls to help me find the cat's owner. You know the town better than I do."

"I'd like to meet all your friends before we leave, Jimmy," his dad said.

Ms. Madden stood up quickly. "I forgot. You haven't met my husband. This is Claudia, Jessi, Mallory, and Nicky. The Baby-sitters Club has been so much help," she added, smiling. "This is my husband — "

"And my dad," Jimmy interrupted.

"James Cook," Ms. Madden finished. "He's adjusted his work schedule so he can help out for the rest of the week."

"I'm glad to meet you," Mallory said. "Jimmy's mentioned you a few times."

Jimmy seemed so much happier with his dad around. He grabbed his father's hand. "Let's take Goldie to the doctor now, please?"

"We'll put up a few signs around the neigh-

74

borhood, describing Goldie. Maybe we can find out who lost her," suggested Jessi.

"And we'll keep our eyes open for any 'lost cat' signs," said Mallory.

"I knew I could count on you," said Ms. Madden.

Mr. Cook looked us all over, after his wife said she could count on us. He raised one eyebrow and shook his head slightly. I don't think he knew any such thing.

CHAPTER 7

"Mrs. O'Neal?" I stood in the doorway of the Kaleidoscope Room, waiting for the woman to turn around.

"Are you Claudia?" she asked when she heard me.

I nodded. "It's nice to meet you, Mrs. O'Neal."

"Nice to meet you finally, Claudia. Come in and see my, I mean, the new Kaleidoscope Room," she said.

"It's great," I replied, meaning it. There was a rainbow of paints on a shelf, colored pencils with new sharp points in a box on the counter, stacks of paper waiting for pictures. Add a little chocolate and it would be perfect.

"I'm not so sure your friend Abby thought it was," Mrs. O'Neal said.

I knew Abby didn't have any complaints about the room. That would have been easy to fix.

"You're the artist, however, and if you think it's okay . . ."

I hated to burst Mrs. O'Neal's bubble, but I was going to have to reinforce Abby's message that the kids needed more freedom with their projects if they were going to want to come to the room. "The room is terrific," I said. "And so are all these supplies. You can do some great projects here."

"And we have space in the hall to serve as a gallery, where the children can display their finished work," Mrs. O'Neal said proudly.

"They'll love that." I took a deep breath. She'd given me my opening. "I taught an art class for awhile. I used to give the kids supplies and let them create something that was uniquely them."

"You mean you let them do anything they wanted to do?" Mrs. O'Neal looked shocked.

"Not exactly. We usually had some guidelines, but sometimes the best projects were the ones that the kids came up with on their own."

"I don't know." She shook her head. "What purpose would that serve?"

"The purpose should be — " I broke off, then tried again. "I think the purpose should be to let children try a lot of different media and discover that art is fun."

"But what will we hang in the gallery?" Mrs. O'Neal said.

"The works they create." I had to wonder why the museum had put Mrs. O'Neal in charge of a kids' art room when it seemed as if she knew so little about working with kids. "It will help them build confidence to see their paintings or sculptures or collages, whatever they make, displayed."

"What if it doesn't look like anything?" Mrs. O'Neal asked.

"They'll still learn something from working with the materials."

"I don't know." Mrs. O'Neal was clutching her pearls, just the way Abby had described.

"Could you give it a try?" I asked.

"It couldn't turn out much worse than the project I planned for last Saturday," Mrs. O'Neal said. "Can you come tomorrow? The room is supposed to open on Friday."

"Tomorrow?" I shook my head. "I can't come tomorrow, but Mary Anne Spier, who helped me with my art classes, can." I'd already cleared this with her. Abby wanted to come too, but I wasn't sure I could sell the idea and Abby at the same time.

"Why can't you make it tomorrow?" Mrs. O'Neal asked.

"I'm baby-sitting. For Rebecca Madden's son."

"Madden? As in Grandmother Madden?" Mrs. O'Neal let go of her pearls.

"The Baby-sitters Club members are helping

get Grandmother Madden's house ready for the sale her family is having this weekend."

"I'm going to that sale. I love Grandmother Madden's work. Have you seen the painting we have here in the museum? It's exquisite," said Mrs. O'Neal.

"I was going to look at it this afternoon. I've heard a lot about her paintings, but I haven't seen one yet," I confessed. I figured I'd probably walked by Grandmother Madden's painting before — I love spending time at the museum — but simply hadn't paid a lot of attention to it.

"It's a pity that Grandmother Madden's work was so underappreciated when she was living," Mrs. O'Neal said sadly. "Her subjects practically invite you to come into the picture, they are so alive."

Talking about Grandmother Madden's work made Mrs. O'Neal come alive too. Her eyes sparkled, the lines on her forehead relaxed, and she used her hands to make her point. Anybody who had this much enthusiasm for art would be a good person to *talk* to kids about it. Maybe the BSC members could help her with the part of her job that involved *working* with kids.

"I always like looking for the cat," she added.

"What cat?" I asked. Was she talking about Goldie?

"Grandmother Madden put a small yellow

cat in each of her paintings. That, the size and shape, and the way her paintings fit together are trademarks of her work," Mrs. O'Neal explained.

Here was something else I didn't know about Grandmother Madden. And what had she meant about the size and shape? "I knew her paintings were small," I said. "Are they all exactly the same size?"

"Each painting is a ten-inch by ten-inch square. And it fits with three other paintings in a series to form a bigger picture."

The last part I already knew. However, I wouldn't be able to see it by looking at just one painting.

"I think I'll try to go see the painting." Mrs. O'Neal had made me excited about Grandmother Madden's work all over again. "Mary Anne will be here tomorrow afternoon with a few of the children we baby-sit for to try out the Kaleidoscope Room again," I added.

"I'd love for you to attend the opening on Friday night," said Mrs. O'Neal. "Maybe you could even help out a little?"

"I'd be glad to," I said, feeling guilty that I hadn't been able to help out before.

"Around seven?"

"See you then." I headed to the gallery before Mrs. O'Neal could ask me to do anything else.

When I found the Grandmother Madden

painting, two people were standing in front of it, blocking my view. I held back, waiting for them to go on, then realized I knew who they were. It was Mr. Ogura and Ms. Madden.

The woman turned her head and looked in my direction. I started to wave but lowered my hand quickly. It wasn't Ms. Madden after all. It was the woman I'd mistaken for her on Monday, the one who'd driven so far to have a look at Grandmother Madden's house. Or so she'd said.

I ducked around the corner before Mr. Ogura saw me, then took another peek. It was amazing how much this woman reminded me of Ms. Madden. They looked more alike than Janine and I do — and we're sisters.

The woman and Mr. Ogura were talking. I tried to hear what they were saying. "Measure," I heard, and peered around the corner to see what they were doing.

Mr. Ogura pulled a tape measure out of his jacket pocket and held it up to the painting. The woman nodded, then pointed at a corner of the painting.

I wanted to hear what they were talking about in the worst way. And it gave me a weird feeling to see them together. Why didn't the woman ask Mr. Ogura to bring her to the house to show her around?

What kind of business was Estates Unlimited?

I'd never heard of it. I filed the question away, planning to look it up in the phone book at home.

Mr. Ogura and the woman backed up a few steps, then turned and walked toward the exit across the room. I waited until they passed through the door, then darted after them. By the time I reached the lobby, they were nowhere in sight.

I took a deep breath, counted to ten, then opened the front door slowly. Mr. Ogura was standing beside his car and the woman was unlocking the door to a gray car. The word "Friday" drifted between the woman and Mr. Ogura. Then she climbed into her car and drove away.

Mr. Ogura sat in his car a few minutes before he pulled out of the parking lot.

I walked back to the gallery, now deserted except for a security guard at the far end. I stood in front of the painting. It was one I recognized from the catalog, an autumn scene with a scarecrow, pumpkins, and some children dressed in Halloween costumes. I moved a little closer and searched the painting inch by inch for . . . Goldie. The golden cat was perched on a front-porch railing belonging to a house much like Grandmother Madden's.

"Excuse me, sir," I said to the guard on duty in the room.

"May I help you?" he asked.

"Do you have a tape measure?" I asked.

He stuck his hands in his pockets, like he wasn't sure whether he'd find one there or not, then shook his head.

"Do you know where I might find one?" Mr. Ogura and the woman had been interested in the measurements of the painting. I decided I'd better know what they were too.

"Maybe at the front desk," he said, scratching his head.

I returned to the lobby and asked the woman at the counter if she had a tape measure.

"Is this for a school project?" she asked me.

"Sort of," I said.

The woman opened a drawer and handed me a yellow tape measure. "Please be sure to bring it back to me when you're finished," she said. "And we close in fifteen minutes."

I looked up at the clock. If I didn't hurry, I'd be late for the BSC meeting. Back in the gallery, I placed the tape against the wall alongside the picture — ten inches by ten inches, just as I'd expected.

I took one last look at the painting, then rolled the tape measure up, and returned it to the woman at the desk.

CHAPTER 8

By the time I returned home from the museum, I was starving. I took a shoe box down from the top shelf of my closet and opened it. I could smell the chocolate even before I tore the wrapping off the Hershey's bar. My mouth was actually watering. I broke it into squares and put three into my mouth at once, letting them melt.

Then I reached for the telephone book under my bed and turned to the business pages. There it was, Estates Unlimited, in bold letters. I picked up the phone to dial the number listed and heard Kristy on the stairs.

"Hi, Claud. I'm starved," she said.

I popped the last chocolate squares in my mouth, then opened a desk drawer and rooted around until I found some Hershey's Kisses. I tossed Kristy a couple and kept a few for myself. I also set out a bag of white cheddar popcorn and some Gummy Bears, in case anyone else was hungry.

"Can you believe that man?" I heard Mary Anne say to Stacey as they ran up the stairs.

"He acted as if it were his house!" Stacey said.

"Who are you talking about?" I asked.

"Mr. Ogura," they said in unison.

"I was so glad when he finally left," said Stacey.

"He was at the Madden house?"

Stacey nodded.

"I saw him at the museum too," I said.

"Did you talk to Mrs. O'Neal?" Abby asked as she burst into the room.

"She's going to try it again," I said. "She wants some kids there tomorrow. I told her you would be there too, Mary Anne. Is that still okay?"

Mary Anne nodded. "I already wrote it down. Abby, are you coming?"

"I was planning on it. I'm supposed to sit for Jamie, and his mom is going to drop us off at the museum."

"Who else might want to go?" Mary Anne asked.

"Go where?" Mal replied. She and Jessi sank down to the floor beside the bed.

"We're going to try something new at the Kaleidoscope Room before it opens on Friday," said Mary Anne.

"Margo might want to go," Mal said. "I

think the rest of the kids have something to do tomorrow. I'll check with Mom and call you." Margo is Mal's seven-year-old sister. If we're not careful, she'll take charge of the Kaleidoscope Room and Mrs. O'Neal all by herself. She's going through a bossy stage these days.

"What about Becca?" Mary Anne asked Jessi.

"Can't. She has a doctor's appointment."

"Corrie is always willing to try an art project," I said.

"She might not be after the last time," said Abby.

"But she has a lot of imagination. I'll call her mom and tell her that it's going to be different this time. And what about Jimmy Cook? He might like to leave his house for a change. And he said he likes to paint."

"How's the cat, by the way?" Mal asked.

"She's doing fine," said Mary Anne. "In fact, she acts as if she's always lived in the house, as queen of the place. Jimmy fixed her a basket to sleep in, and they bought her some food. She won't let anyone pass by without petting her. It's so funny! She meows and sticks her head under your hand. Goldie is almost as sweet as Tigger."

"Has anyone called? The owner? Jessi and I hung up signs all over the neighborhood," said Mal.

"If anyone called, Ms. Madden didn't say

anything about it, but she was only there for a few minutes," Mary Anne reported. "She said she had to go to a meeting at the estate sale place."

"Estates Unlimited?" I asked, sitting up.

"I think that was the name," said Stacey.

"But you said Mr. Ogura was at the house."

"He arrived soon after we did," said Mary Anne. "And right after Ms. Madden left. He said he forgot where they were supposed to meet, but that didn't keep him from sticking around to bother us. All the books that Jessi and I had sorted and shelved were mixed up and spread all over the library. When I said something to Mr. Ogura about it, he said I better get busy then, because it was only a few days until the sale. Can you believe it? I saw him come out of the library right before I went in and found the mess."

"I saw Mr. Ogura at the museum around four-thirty. When was he meeting with Ms. Madden?" I picked up the telephone and dialed it.

"What are you doing?" Kristy asked. "A client might be trying to call us."

I put my forefinger to my lips. The phone rang a few times, then an answering machine picked up. "Estates Unlimited," said a woman's voice. "I'm sorry but our office is closed for the evening. Please call back tomorrow between the hours of ten and five. We'll be looking forward to talking to you." I hung up.

"Who are you calling?" Kristy wanted to know.

"Estates Unlimited, to see if Mr. Ogura really works there. He's always trying to get inside to look around the Madden house, saying that he works for the company, but why doesn't he have a key? And who was Rebecca meeting with if Mr. Ogura was at the house? Also, you know what? When I saw him at the museum today, he was with that woman who came to the house wanting to get in early. Remember her, Kristy? The one who looked sort of like Ms. Madden?"

"Yeah, I remember. She left before Ms. Madden had a chance to talk to her."

"She wasn't at the house today, was she?" I asked Mary Anne.

"The only other person who came by was a deliveryman," said Stacey. "But that turned out kind of weird too."

"What do you mean?" I leaned in closer.

Stacey sighed. "This deliveryman, who didn't really look like a deliveryman . . ."

"Meaning?" I wanted to know every detail.

"Meaning he didn't have any pizza?" Abby asked.

Stacey ignored her. "He was very good-looking and he was dressed in a navy blue blazer and khaki pants, wearing a tie. That's pretty dressed up for most of the deliverymen I've seen. Anyway, he dropped off some big, flat packages wrapped in brown paper and said to be sure that Ms. Madden got them. When she came home at about a quarter to five, I showed her the packages and asked if I should unpack them. She said no, really fast, then said we'd worked hard enough for one day and it was time for us to go. You know, I think there were paintings or pictures in those packages. It reminded me of the way you wrap up your paintings, Claud."

"Paintings?" My ears perked up. I remembered Ms. Madden talking on the telephone the first day, promising to get some paintings to someone. "How big were they?"

"Big," said Stacey. "The man was staggering as he carried them inside."

They weren't Grandmother Madden's work, then. All her paintings, I now knew, were less than a foot square. Even if there were four of them put together the painting wouldn't be very big. "What kind of delivery truck?" I asked.

"I didn't see the truck," Stacey said. "But another thing about Mr. Ogura — when he came downstairs, I noticed that he had flakes of paint all over his pants. But he's an appraiser, not a contractor."

"Hmm," I said. "I know we haven't learned anything that would prove Grandmother Madden didn't destroy her paintings," I continued, "but there's also nothing to say that she did."

"Except that there aren't any paintings," Abby reminded me.

"Well, no one's been able to find them. I keep trying to bring up the idea that the paintings still exist, but Ms. Madden doesn't want to talk about it. And one day I heard her say to someone on the phone that she couldn't deliver the paintings she'd promised because there was a problem. She wouldn't let me touch a painting loaded into the trunk of her car, and she wouldn't let Stacey unpack the paintings that came today. Plus, she couldn't have met with Mr. Ogura today. When did *he* have time? He was at the house, then at the museum this afternoon. Did Ms. Madden mention that she'd missed Mr. Ogura?"

"She didn't say anything at all about what she was doing while she was gone," said Stacey.

"You know, it's not just you, Stacey. Mr. Ogura gives me the creeps too," said Mary Anne.

Okay. That was it. Mary Anne is always the last one to say anything bad about anybody.

"He sneaks around the house and watches everybody," she continued. "He always wants to see Ms. Madden, but I've never seen them together."

"Claudia, remember that day he had a telephone call at the Maddens'? He left the phone off the hook when he was finished. Maybe it wasn't an accident. Maybe he didn't want anybody else to call," Kristy said. "If he's not who he says he is, then he wouldn't want to talk to someone who wanted to talk to Mr. Ogura."

"I'm going to call Estates Unlimited again, as soon as I can. We'll see whether he really works for them or not," I said, resolving to know the answer before the next BSC meeting.

"Don't forget about the woman who showed up at the door, then disappeared," said Kristy.

"Only to turn up at the museum with Mr. Ogura," I said. "We need to keep our eyes open for her. She said she'd driven a hundred miles for the estate sale. But if Mr. Ogura works for the estate company, why doesn't he bring the woman with him to see the house?"

"And what about Jimmy's dad?" Stacey asked.

"Yeah, there is something weird about him," I said. "He doesn't want Ms. Madden to go to art school, for one thing. Jimmy said his dad doesn't want his mom to paint. In fact, Jimmy likes to paint, but doesn't want to tell his dad because he's afraid his dad will get mad at him. If any of you happen to see Mr. Cook around the house, pay attention to what he says and does. I'd like to know what's up with him."

"He was very nice to Goldie," Mal said. "And Jimmy adores his dad."

"Jimmy's been a different kid since his dad arrived," I agreed.

Kristy was clearly thinking about something else. "Have you had a chance to look at the paintings in the studio?" she asked. "Can we match them to that list of paintings Mary Anne found?"

"I haven't had a chance to work in the studio since Mr. Cook arrived," I replied, "but I know that the paintings in there are student work. They don't have any connection to the list Mary Anne found."

"Where is that list of paintings?" Mary Anne asked. "Maybe we need to find out how many paintings are actually missing."

"I don't know where the original is, but I have a copy of it that I found on the stairs." I'd stuck the list in the pocket of my jeans and forgotten about it until Mary Anne mentioned it. "Some of the paintings have been crossed out and check marks have been made by others. I wanted to try to figure out what it all meant, but I haven't had much time. Maybe I can stop by the library tomorrow and do some research."

"What about the catalog that was with the list? Can we use it to find out what we want to know?" Stacey asked.

"If we could find it, we might be able to," I said.

"That's something we could do while we're working at the Madden house," said Mal. "Look for the catalog."

"And try to talk to Mr. Cook," said Kristy.

"And this is something else I really want to know — where's that portrait of the Japanese woman I saw the first day?" I asked. "It was in the studio one minute, then when I came back it was gone. Nobody else even remembers seeing it."

"We've all been looking for that," said Jessi, "but I haven't seen anything like it."

"Claudia, do you think Ms. Madden has some of her grandmother's paintings hidden someplace?" Abby asked.

"I don't know," I admitted. "If she does, it would definitely explain some of her suspicious behavior. All right. We'll try talking to Ms. Madden, Mr. Cook, and Mr. Ogura. And I'll try to find out more about Estates Unlimited and exactly where the existing Grandmother Madden paintings are," I said.

"All this and sorting too!" said Abby. "Who knew that baby-sitting at the Maddens would be such a big job?" She flopped on my floor in fake exhaustion. "I'm almost looking forward to working at the museum tomorrow."

I threw a Gummy Bear at her.

She was right, though. It was a lot of work. And with the sale only three days away, we didn't have much time.

CHAPTER 9

Thursday

It seems as if sometimes we solve one problem just in time for another one to come up. Take the Kaleidoscope Room. We'd convinced Mrs. O'Neal to try a new way of doing things, but it may have worked out a little too well. The kids are taking their artwork very seriously.

I wasn't surprised when Mary Anne told me that the "new" Kaleidoscope Room was a big hit with the kids. But I was a little surprised to hear how much Abby had gotten into the spirit of things.

Mary Anne, Abby, and Jamie arrived a little before the rest of the group. Mrs. O'Neal let them into the room, then left.

"You think she's mad?" Abby asked.

"From what Claudia said, I think she doesn't want to see anything messed up," said Mary Anne.

"Where's the clay?" Jamie asked. "I want to make some more snakes."

Mary Anne opened cabinet doors until she found the clay in a large plastic bucket. She took out a hunk and placed it on the table in front of Jamie. "Here you go. Make lots of snakes."

"I want to paint them too," he said. "I want a green snake and a black snake and a copper-head. I have a whole book about snakes at home and I know what they look like. Can I paint them, please?"

"We can probably work something out," Mary Anne said.

"Do you think the kids who want to make pictures have to paint on the tables?" Abby asked. "Can't they use these easels?"

"Sure. Why?" asked Mary Anne.

"Last time Mrs. O'Neal wanted them to paint at the tables," Abby explained. "I know I'm the only one here who's allergic to paint, but keeping the paints close to the windows and keeping the windows open will mean I don't get so stuffed up."

Mary Anne hung paper on each easel, while Abby opened windows, then filled baby food jars with different colors of paint, placing a brush in each jar.

Abby picked up a brush that stood in a jar of red paint. She made a few dots on the paper. She put that brush back and picked up the one from the jar of blue paint. She drew a fat blue line around the red dots. "I haven't done this in years," she said, adding more colors.

Mary Anne found safety scissors, paste, and colored paper and set them out on another table. "There's lots of good stuff here," she said. "I bet the kids will really have fun today."

"Hmmm?" said Abby, intent on her painting.

"Never mind," Mary Anne said. She turned to greet Ms. Madden and Jimmy. "I'm so glad you could come." Jimmy stood behind his mother.

"Jimmy loves to paint," Ms. Madden said.

"But my daddy doesn't like it," said Jimmy in a low voice.

"Daddy doesn't mind if you come here and

make pictures," Ms. Madden said with a laugh.

"But he told you — "

"Really, Jimmy, it's okay." Ms. Madden ushered him into the room. "There's clay and easels and some colored paper here. What would you like to do?"

Mary Anne slipped an apron over Jimmy's head.

"I want to paint," said Jimmy, going straight to the easel beside Abby.

"I'll be back for him in about an hour," said Ms. Madden. "He does love to paint."

"We'll let him paint all he wants to," said Mary Anne. Whether his dad likes it or not, she thought.

Mrs. Pike dropped off Margo, who headed for the clay table, where Jamie was seated.

Corrie's mom waved to Mary Anne, then disappeared. Corrie paused in the doorway.

"Hi, Corrie." Mary Anne greeted her. "What do you feel like doing today?"

"Do I have to paint somebody else's picture?" Corrie asked in a low voice.

"You may paint anything you want," Mary Anne assured her.

"Okay, then I'll paint," said Corrie.

Mary Anne helped her with her apron. "Abby, Corrie would like to paint," she said.

"Just a minute," Abby said. "I'm almost finished with this picture." Hanging out to dry on the line next to Abby was a row of pictures, de-signs mostly, in a variety of colors. The one she was working on was done entirely in blue.

"Abby?" Mary Anne said gently. "May Corrie have a turn?"

Abby removed her blue painting from the easel and hung it on the line to dry. "That was fun," she said.

Mary Anne hung a sheet of paper on the easel for Corrie. Corrie picked up a brush and started to outline a person. Abby stood beside her.

Mary Anne felt a tug on her shirt. "What do you need, Jamie?" she asked.

"We want to paint our snakes now," he said.

"Abby, can you find some newspaper to put on the table, so that Jamie and Margo can paint the clay?" Mary Anne asked.

Abby continued to watch Corrie paint.

"Abby?" Mary Anne repeated.

"What?" Abby asked, finally looking at Mary Anne.

"Jamie and Margo need some help painting their clay," Mary Anne pointed out.

"No problem," Abby said. "What do you want me to do?"

"Find newspaper to cover the table," Mary Anne said.

Abby nodded, then started looking through the cabinets.

"I need brown and green and black," said Jamie.

"I want blue and red," said Margo.

"There's no such thing as a blue-and-red snake," said Jamie.

"This is a snake out of a fairy story. It's a good snake and it's really a princess," said Margo. "But somebody has to kiss it first."

"Not me," said Jamie.

Mary Anne turned back to the easels.

"I'm finished with this one," said Jimmy.

"Jimmy, that's a terrific painting," Mary Anne said. "It looks a little like a Van Gogh." Jimmy's painting was of a big yellow flower surrounded by a lot of trees. The flower was bigger than any of the trees.

"I'm going to paint my cat, Goldie, next," he said.

"I'm finished with this painting," Corrie called out. "I want to do another one."

Mary Anne gave her a new sheet of paper. "These dancers remind me of Degas," she said. "He painted pictures of ballet dancers and he also made sculptures of ballerinas."

Corrie smiled broadly and started in on her next painting.

Before long, the drying lines were filled with paintings by Abby, Jimmy, and Corrie.

"Do you think they'll choose one of these to hang in the gallery?" Corrie asked Mary Anne.

"I'm sure of it."

"Where should I put this snake?" Jamie called out. "There's no more room on the table."

He was right. The table was covered with snakes of all shapes, colors, and sizes, and Margo was busy making yet another snake princess.

Abby spread newspaper on a second table and moved some of the snakes to it.

"How is it going in here?" Mrs. O'Neal asked from the doorway.

"Fun!" Jamie said.

The other children continued to paint.

"It's quiet and the work is very good," said Mrs. O'Neal, sounding surprised. She finally came into the room and walked along the line of paintings. "This doesn't look like it was done by a young child at all." She pointed at Corrie's painting of the dancers.

Corrie's cheeks flushed as she painted a pink skirt on yet another ballerina.

"I'm amazed at what these children can do. Look at this flower! It looks so real I want to pick it. And those snakes . . . are you sure they won't bite?" asked Mrs. O'Neal.

Mary Anne and Abby exchanged smiles while Margo and Jamie beamed.

"Regular little Michelangelos, these children are," said Mrs. O'Neal. "We'll have a good beginning for our Kaleidoscope Gallery. In fact, I don't know how I'm going to choose."

Corrie looked up, panic on her face.

"A few of each," suggested Mary Anne, patting Corrie's shoulder.

"I'll be just like my great-grandmother," said Jimmy. "She has a painting hanging in this museum too."

"Your great-grandmother is an artist?" said Mrs. O'Neal.

"Grandmother Madden," said Jimmy. "And my mom paints pictures too. Can I take this picture of Goldie home to show my mom?"

"A cat, just like in your great-grandmother's paintings," said Mrs. O'Neal. "That's wonderful, just wonderful."

"I'll leave it up to you girls to choose which paintings and which sculptures to display," Mrs. O'Neal continued. "You've done such a good job, how would you like to work with the Kaleidoscope Program? The room will be open after school and on Saturdays. I could use you. I didn't think letting the children decide on their own projects would be a good idea, but it seems to have worked very well indeed."

"I'd like to help out sometimes," said Abby.

"I would too," said Mary Anne.

"I need a lot of hands for the opening on Friday night," Mrs. O'Neal said. "Do you think you could come then? Claudia has already agreed to be here."

"We could probably bring a few more people too, if you want. I bet some of the other members of the Baby-sitters Club would help out," said Mary Anne.

"Come around seven and we'll set up. Now, be sure to clean up before you close the room," said Mrs. O'Neal. "And don't forget to hang some of these wonderful paintings and display some of the sculptures to show people what we do in our program."

"Is the hall the only place we can display the work?" Mary Anne asked.

"You may use the entire hall," Mrs. O'Neal said. "There were some screens too."

"Where are they?" Mary Anne asked, hoping that might solve the space problem.

"I put them in this closet," said Mrs. O'Neal, crossing the room and opening the door to a storage area.

"Okay, great," said Mary Anne.

"Don't forget to clean up in here before you leave," Mrs. O'Neal reminded them again as she exited, a cloud of flowery perfume lingering in the air.

"Okay, cleanup time," said Mary Anne. "Your parents will be here soon to pick you guys up. Finish what you're working on now and then go wash your hands."

"Are you going to hang any of my paintings?" Corrie asked Abby.

"Of course. You're as good as . . ." Abby glanced at Mary Anne, then said quickly, "Pele."

"Who?" asked Corrie.

Mrs. Addison appeared at the door. "Corrie, are you ready to go home?"

Corrie looked from her mother to Abby.

Abby noticed Mrs. Addison glancing at her watch. "Quick, wash your hands," said Abby. "We'll see you Friday night at the opening."

Looking at the kids' paintings, Abby was sure it would be an exhibition the Stoneybrook Museum would *never* forget.

CHAPTER 10

"Did you have a good time at the Kaleidoscope Room?" I asked Jimmy when I ran into him later at the Maddens'. I'd been worried about how things would work out and was glad to see that Jimmy had a smile on his face.

"I painted this picture of Goldie," he said, holding it up for me to see. "Mary Anne and Abby are going to hang some of my pictures in the gallery, just like Great-granny's. And my dad is going to go see them. Mom promised."

"That's terrific!" I admired the cat. It was very good. Jimmy had captured the contented expression Goldie had developed since she'd moved into the Maddens'.

"Where is Goldie? I want her to see her picture," said Jimmy.

"Last time I saw her, she was in her basket in the kitchen, napping," I said. I took Jimmy by the hand and led him through the hallway.

He knelt beside the cat and showed her the

picture he'd painted. "I'm going to hang it right here." He held it against the refrigerator.

"Here, Jimmy," said Kristy. She tore off a few pieces of tape from a roll on the counter and stuck the picture to the side of the refrigerator, down low where the cat could see it.

"Is Stacey still around?" I asked. We'd all been working so hard that I hadn't seen anyone else since we'd arrived.

"She's gone, but Mary Anne took her place in the library," said Kristy.

I wanted to talk to Mary Anne about the Kaleidoscope Room, but there was still a lot to do in the studio. I didn't want to lose any time that I had to work up there. "Want to go up to the studio and help me decide which paints to throw away?" I asked Jimmy.

He nodded, gave Goldie one last pat, then ran ahead of me up the stairs.

I made a side trip into one of the bedrooms to pick up a large trash can I'd seen there earlier. As I pulled it along, I heard something knock against the side. An empty plastic garbage bag was lining the can, so I pulled it loose to see what was under it. And there was the Japanese portrait I'd been searching for. I pulled it out, balanced it on an easel, and gazed at it. The woman's secret smile still intrigued me.

I felt Jimmy's hand in mine. He leaned his

head against my waist and said in a muffled voice, "Please don't tell my mom."

"Tell her what?" I knelt beside him and put my arm around him. He hid his face in my shoulder and I felt tears soak through my cotton shirt.

"It was an accident," he said. "I didn't mean to knock it over."

"Jimmy, I don't know what you're talking about."

"I came up here to look for Mom that day, and the painting fell over. I picked it up and . . ." His finger touched the surface of the portrait.

Then I saw what he was upset about. There was a chip in the textured background of the painting. I looked a little closer. "That's not such a big deal," I assured him. "I think it can be fixed." If I had a chance to buy the portrait, that's exactly what I'd do. But for now, I decided I better leave it alone. I wanted to study the painting to learn more about its texture anyway. "Has the painting been in the trash can all this time?" I asked.

Jimmy shook his head. "I stuck it in the cabinet over there, with the other paintings. But then I got worried that somebody would find it."

"What cabinet? What other paintings?" I felt a fluttering in my stomach. I walked to the wall

Jimmy pointed out. Some paintings were leaning against it. I moved them out of the way. The wall was paneled, and I had to look hard to see the door and the tiny latch because it looked like another seam in the wood. I pulled the door open and the fluttering in my stomach became a full-fledged churning. Lots more paintings were inside . . . and some of them were small squares, about the size of Grandmother Madden's. I pulled them out one by one, and the churning died down as each canvas turned out to be the work of a student.

But the last painting made me pause. It was a small square, and it was done in the primitive style with figures that reminded me of a Grandmother Madden. Yet something about it — the colors, for one thing — lacked the vibrancy of Grandmother Madden's. I decided that I better show it to Ms. Madden anyway. It could be from an experiment, an attempt at something new by her grandmother. The picture captured my attention the same way a Madden did. There was every bit as much to see in it as there'd been in the painting I'd studied at the museum.

"I want to show this to your mom," I said to Jimmy.

"Are you going to tell her about the other picture?" Jimmy asked, worry lines forming a crease between his eyebrows.

"We'll just show her this one now," I said. I knew I'd have to show her the damaged painting eventually, but I didn't think I had to do it that minute. "Do you want to come with me?"

"I think I'll go play with Goldie," he answered, and zipped out the door.

I tucked the painting under my arm and headed toward the library to see if I could find Ms. Madden. As soon as I took one step into the hall, I wished I could turn around and shut the studio doors. Mr. Ogura was standing in front of me. I can't begin to describe the look on his face when he saw the painting I was holding.

"What do you have there?" he asked, reaching for it in slow motion.

I turned it and held it against my chest. I didn't want to show it to him before Ms. Madden had a chance to see it.

"Let me see," he said, walking toward me as I moved backward. I stumbled against the doorjamb behind me.

"I'd like Ms. Madden to see it first," I said.

Mr. Ogura's eyes narrowed and his hand remained outstretched.

I clutched the painting more tightly.

"I don't think Ms. Madden is home right now," Mr. Ogura said. "Let me show it to her when she returns. I'm sure she'll want an expert opinion on it. No doubt Rebecca will want me to take it into the office to show it to one of our art experts."

I shook my head. "I want Ms. Madden to see it first," I repeated. I wondered if he, too, thought the painting might be a Madden. Why else would he be so interested in it?

In the next instant Mr. Ogura pulled the picture out of my arms, leaving me empty-handed and openmouthed.

"I want to see this in better light." He moved into the hallway.

I stayed close to him, like a shadow.

"Claudia! Claudia, come here a minute," Mary Anne called from the foot of the front staircase.

"Go ahead," Mr. Ogura said.

I hesitated.

"Claudia, I have something you'll want to see," Mary Anne called again.

"I'll be right back," I said to Mr. Ogura. "Please don't take that painting anyplace."

I ran down the steps and into the library. "What?" I asked Mary Anne breathlessly, looking over my shoulder to see if Mr. Ogura had followed with the painting.

Mary Anne held up a color photograph of a cat that looked like Goldie. "Behind the photo was something you'll like even more," she said, handing me a small painting. I saw the cat again, painted in oils and signed "Rebecca."

"The cat," I whispered. "I didn't check for the cat! Mary Anne, I'll be right back." I carried the painted cat with me as I hurried back to the studio.

"Claudia, how's it going?" Ms. Madden ran up the back steps just as I ran up the front steps.

"Ms. Madden, you're home! I found a painting. You have to see it. Mr. Ogura has it in here." I pushed open the studio doors. Funny, I was sure I'd left them open when I'd gone downstairs a few minutes before.

"Mr. Ogura?" Ms. Madden looked puzzled. "I thought he was going to Japan this week. But maybe I was wrong. Maybe he's going next week."

My mind's eye flashed back to the airline tickets I'd seen in Mr. Ogura's car earlier in the week. They were for Japan Airlines, I remembered. Maybe the guy *was* okay. I hadn't had a chance to call Estates Unlimited yet. At any rate, he wasn't in the studio and neither was the painting. I looked out the window, but his car was nowhere in sight. Maybe he'd parked in front. I whirled around, then ran back the way I'd come, leaving a surprised Ms. Madden behind.

I heard a sickening thud as I rounded the corner at the bottom of the staircase. Mr. Ogura wasn't in sight, but the painting had been leaning against the newel post and when I flew by it, I knocked it over. Slowly, I picked it up and turned it over, hoping I hadn't caused any irreparable damage. A few flakes of paint drifted off as I turned it right side up, but otherwise it seemed okay.

A shadow fell over me, and I expected to see Ms. Madden when I looked up. Instead, I saw Mr. Cook, frowning as usual.

"What have you done now?" he asked in his deep voice.

"I was looking for this painting and when I walked by," I cleared my throat, "it fell over."

He grabbed the painting out of my hands. "Where did you find this? This could be very valuable," he said. "My wife must be out of her mind to let a bunch of kids handle these things." He turned his back on me and started up the steps.

"I wanted to check something," I said, reaching out.

"No one but an appraiser is going to check anything," said Mr. Cook. "I'm not sure you understand how valuable some of Rebecca's grandmother's things may be," he added in a softer tone. "We appreciate your help with Jimmy and with all the sorting, but there are some things that you need to leave to those who know something about art and antiques."

Mr. Cook held the painting carefully as he

climbed the stairs. I expected to see him turn toward the studio, but he disappeared into a bedroom, shutting the door firmly behind him.

Did he suspect the painting was a Madden too? I followed him upstairs, deciding to show Ms. Madden the cat painting. After all, I'd said I had something to show her. I'd have to leave the news about the maybe-Madden to Mr. Cook.

It would be fun to line up a row of cats — to see one of Grandmother Madden's cats beside Ms. Madden's painting and the painting of Goldie Jimmy had done at the Kaleidoscope Room.

The studio was empty once again. Where had Ms. Madden gone now? I placed the small cat picture on a table and started throwing away old paints.

My mind was churning. Could that painting possibly be a Madden — one that had been overlooked all this time? Mr. Cook and Mr. Ogura had certainly been interested in it. I didn't dare believe it, myself. But I couldn't quite keep from hoping.

CHAPTER 11

"We're finished!" Ms. Madden sat on the bottom step of the front staircase, her arms around her knees, after we'd priced the last cup and sorted the last book. It was Friday afternoon. "I couldn't have done it without your help."

"I had a good time," I said. "And I'm looking forward to the sale tomorrow."

"You're going to help then too, aren't you?" Ms. Madden asked.

"I wouldn't miss it."

"I need to get cleaned up for the big exhibit opening." Ms. Madden stood and brushed off her jeans. "Jimmy is very excited that he'll have a picture in the same museum as his great-grandmother."

"Maybe you'll have one there too someday," I said, hoping the same thing for myself.

"If this sale turns out okay and I can put the money together for art school." She sighed. "Then no one will stop me."

I wanted to ask her about the painting I'd found the day before, but I didn't know what Mr. Cook had done with it. I didn't want to cause any trouble. I'd looked all around the house as I worked that afternoon, and I hadn't seen the painting I'd been calling a maybe-Madden anyplace. If it were a Madden, I decided, someone would have mentioned it. "I'll see you tonight, then," I said, opening the front door.

"Thanks again for all your help," Ms. Madden said.

My hope of finding a Madden painting was fading fast. Between cleaning, sorting, and pricing, we'd turned over everything in that house. All we'd found that was even close was the one painting. I needed to let go of my notion of a secret store of Madden paintings and just be glad that we'd helped Ms. Madden and had fun sitting for Jimmy.

I decided to drop by the library to pick up the books on primitive art that I'd reserved earlier. Mom had said she'd bring them home, but I knew if I waited for her to do that I wouldn't have a chance to look at them before I left for the Kaleidoscope Room opening.

"Claudia, you're back!" My mom wore the same surprised expression that she'd had on when I'd showed up the week before.

"I came to look at the books on primitive art," I explained.

"Here you go." Mom reached under the counter and handed them to me. "I would have brought them home with me, you know."

"Couldn't wait," I said, carrying them to a table nearby.

In the biggest book was a whole chapter on Grandmother Madden. I took the copy of the list I found out of my pocket and compared it to the paintings mentioned. Pretty soon, I noticed a pattern. The paintings with check marks by the names were in museums, and the paintings with lines drawn through them were owned by individuals, including members of the Madden family. I almost swallowed my tongue when I read who else owned an original Grandmother Madden — D. Ogura. Mr. Ogura owned a Madden?

I slammed the book shut. It was only 4:15. I could still make it to Estates Unlimited before closing time.

I had a stitch in my side by the time I reached the office building where Estates Unlimited was located. Inside were a sofa and some plants and a very blonde, very pretty receptionist.

"I'd like to talk to Mr. Ogura," I said.

"Now, would that be old Mr. Ogura or young Mr. Ogura?" the woman asked me.

116

Two Mr. Oguras? I stammered a little as I tried to figure out what to answer. The Mr. Ogura I was looking for had to be "young Mr. Ogura." He didn't look old enough to have a son of his own. Unless, of course, he wasn't "Mr. Ogura" at all. "Young Mr. Ogura," I finally answered.

The receptionist picked up the phone and punched in some numbers. She waited a moment, then smiled at me. She had the whitest teeth I'd ever seen. "I'm sorry, but Mr. Ogura doesn't answer. He must have left for the day. May I tell Dale who stopped by to see him?"

I shook my head, my ponytail sweeping back and forth. "I'll, uh, speak with him later."

"Have a good afternoon," the woman said pleasantly.

I pushed the door open and almost knocked Mr. Cook over.

"You!" he said.

"I'm really sorry," I apologized, then held the door while he rushed into the office. He was carrying the maybe-Madden! I thought for about one second about not saying anything, but I couldn't stop myself. "Why are you bringing that here? Have you shown the picture to Ms. Madden yet?"

"I'm having it appraised. I told you we were going to do that."

Even though he sounded cross, as usual, I

felt a bit sorry for him. Mr. Cook didn't look comfortable. Estates Unlimited was probably the last place he wanted to be.

I couldn't very well follow him back inside, so I let the door close. I watched through the glass door as he said something to the receptionist. She showed him into a back office. I decided to wait awhile to see what he found out.

There was a wooden bench nearby. Sitting there, I could see the door, but no one inside could see me watching. I sifted through my thoughts about the goings-on at Grandmother Madden's house.

All my ideas hinged on my feeling that Grandmother Madden hadn't destroyed her paintings. If she hadn't, they still existed someplace — and the most likely place was in her house. I'd looked and looked and hadn't found anything except one painting that was a maybe-Madden. I was sure that Ms. Madden had looked every bit as hard as I had, even though she claimed she didn't believe there were any Grandmother Maddens left. And, it certainly seemed as if Mr. Ogura was doing the same thing.

I caught a flash of red out of the corner of my eye — Mr. Ogura's Mercedes. I pretended to be looking through my backpack, hoping that he wouldn't notice it was me sitting outside his office. But he drove past. I looked up in time to see two people in the car. Mr. Ogura was driving, but I couldn't make out the other person. I couldn't even tell if it was a man or a woman.

I slung my backpack over my shoulder. I was cold, and if I didn't hurry up, I would be late for the BSC meeting. Maybe my friends could help me make some sense of this mystery. I didn't feel as though I were making any progress, and we were just about out of time.

Mallory was the last of my friends to arrive at our BSC meeting. The rest of us were already talking about the happenings at the Madden house. I had told everybody about finding the maybe-Madden, and losing it to Mr. Cook, and how I hadn't seen it this afternoon, as Ms. Madden and I had finished preparing for the sale.

"Ms. Madden said that if the estate sale was a success, she'd have the money for art school," I said, repeating a part of my earlier conversation.

"Maybe that's why Mr. Cook is so grumpy," said Mary Anne.

"Why would that make him grumpy?" I asked. "It would make Ms. Madden grumpier."

"He might feel as though he's the husband, so he should be able to pay for school for his wife," Mary Anne explained. "Some guys are like that."

"Or he could think it was a waste of time. Jimmy said something like that the first time we talked about it," I said.

"It's not a waste of time if she's talented," said Jessi.

I didn't think art school was a waste of time under any circumstances.

"Anyway, I ran into Mr. Cook at Estates Unlimited this afternoon," I announced.

"Talking to Mr. Ogura?" Stacey asked.

"He was taking the maybe-Madden in to have it appraised," I said. "And I learned one thing: Mr. Ogura does work at Estates Unlimited. In fact, there are two of them at the company, father and son."

The looks on the faces of my friends reflected the look I must have had when the receptionist told me there were two Mr. Oguras.

"The young Mr. Ogura, the one we've met, is named Dale. He was out of the office when I was there. I saw him in his car with someone else right after I left Mr. Cook."

"Mr. Cook was with Mr. Ogura?" Mal asked.

"No, he was still in the office. I couldn't see who was in the car with Mr. Ogura," I admitted.

"So our Mr. Ogura is who he says he is. But that's all we managed to find out," said Kristy.

"I had a chance to go to the library and check the list of paintings against a reference book on primitive art. I found out something pretty interesting," I said, drawing out the announcement. "The paintings with check marks beside them are owned by museums. The ones with lines drawn through them belong to individuals, including people in the Madden family. The big news is that D. Ogura owns a Madden painting."

I was disappointed that no one reacted more dramatically. The surprised looks were good, but not as good as gasps.

"Do you think that's Dale Ogura?" Abby asked. "Isn't he young to collect expensive art?"

"When I found out D. Ogura owned a painting, I immediately thought of our Mr. Ogura. But since there's another Mr. Ogura, I thought it could be Dale's father."

"You know, some other paintings are missing too," said Stacey. "I've never seen the paintings that were delivered on Wednesday again. I've been thinking. If Ms. Madden found some of her grandmother's paintings, she wouldn't have to worry about money. But she might have to share any money from the paintings with her cousins. If they knew."

"So that would explain why she's hiding the Grandmother Maddens — if that's what's going on," I said.

Stacey shrugged. "She's so nice that I don't want to think that, but it makes sense."

I had to admit it did. Ms. Madden needed money, she had the best opportunity to find the paintings, and she seemed to be hiding something. All of this was based on the assumption that there were paintings to be found.

"And they're Ms. Madden's paintings anyway," said Kristy. "Her grandmother left her the house and its contents."

Kristy had brought up something that I hadn't thought about before. What if Ms. Madden had already found the paintings? They were hers. I sighed. "Be sure to look at Grandmother Madden's painting at the museum tonight when we're there," I said. "It might be the only one you'll ever see."

CHAPTER 12

Friday

When Mrs. Addison called and asked me to take Corrie to the opening of the Kaleidoscope Room, my first thought was that Corrie was going to be very disappointed that her parents were not going to be at the opening. Give me one cup of disappointment mixed with one cup of mad, and I'll give you somebody who's no fun. Of course, I didn't know at first that something else was bothering Corrie even more than her mother not coming to see her pictures.

Stacey and Corrie were the first ones to arrive at the museum for the opening. They had to wait for Mrs. O'Neal to unlock the Kaleidoscope Room. Mr. and Mrs. Addison had dropped them off on their way to a dinner party, with a promise to return later. I know that Stacey tried hard to cheer Corrie up. If she'd known the whole story she could have helped Corrie sooner.

While they were waiting for the room to open, Stacey admired the paintings that hung in the Kaleidoscope Gallery. "Look at these great pictures!" Stacey said. "Which are yours?"

Corrie had tears glistening in her eyes as she pulled her ballerina pictures off the wall. "These are awful. I don't want anyone to see them. And I'm never going to paint again. Ever."

Stacey grabbed the paintings before Corrie could crumple them. "I like them," she said.

Corrie shook her head and sat on the floor, her back against the wall, eyes looking toward the ceiling. "I didn't want to come, but my mom made me. It's a good thing I did or everyone would have seen these paintings. They're horrible."

"Why do you think they're horrible?" Stacey had studied the pictures and was sure she couldn't paint a ballerina as well as Corrie had.

"They just are," Corrie answered. "And somebody told me I was a bad painter."

Stacey sat on the floor, putting herself between Corrie and her paintings. "Do you want to tell me who this person is who told you such a thing?"

"No. I don't want to talk about it anymore." Corrie picked up Stacey's hand. "I like these pictures on your fingernails. Did you paint them?"

Stacey shook her head. "Those are decals that I bought and stuck on top of the nail polish. I wish I'd taken time to redo the polish underneath, though. It's chipping and I'll have to take the decals off before I can take the polish off."

"Do you have any more? I want some on my fingernails too," said Corrie.

Stacey opened her purse. She pulled out a calculator, a billfold, some papers, lipstick, a hairbrush, and finally a small package of decals. "I was going to give these to Claud, but I bet she wouldn't mind if you used some of them."

"Look, there's my snake!" Margo Pike appeared, pulling Mallory toward Stacey and Corrie. She was pointing at the display case in the Kaleidoscope Gallery that was filled with snakes of different colors and sizes.

"Where's the rest of your family?" Stacey asked Mallory, as she carefully applied a decal on top of Corrie's fingernail. The nail had some polish on it already. (As Stacey told me later, it had definitely been applied sometime in the past year.) There was a little blob in the center of the nail. Stacey was trying to affix the decal there.

"They're coming, but Margo couldn't wait. She wanted to be here when the place opened."

Abby and Mary Anne waved from the end of the hall.

"Hi, Corrie," Mary Anne greeted her. "How does it feel to be a published artist? I guess that's not exactly the word. What is it when an artist has art hanging in a gallery?" Abby, Mallory, and Stacey giggled with her, but nobody could figure out what word Mary Anne was looking for.

"You're a published artist too," Corrie said to Abby.

Abby walked past Corrie and found one of the designs she'd painted. Mrs. O'Neal had hung it, even though it wasn't one Abby and Mary Anne had selected. "I can't believe it. This is one of my pictures."

"How *does* it feel to be a published artist?" Stacey asked, setting off a new storm of giggles.

"Corrie, your ballerina paintings are better than my design," Abby said. "Where are they?"

"They're right here," Stacey answered. "Corrie doesn't want them displayed."

"Why not? They're excellent," said Abby.

"You said they were awful," said Corrie, tears welling in her eyes again.

"I didn't!" said Abby.

Corrie turned away. "I asked my brother if he knew who Pele was and he said Pele was a soccer player. He doesn't paint at all."

Stacey saw Abby swallow hard.

"What I meant," Abby said, kneeling beside Corrie, "is that you're as good at art as Pele is at soccer. I was trying to think of a way to give you a compliment, but I didn't know how. I'm sorry if you misunderstood what I meant."

"Then who do I paint like?" Corrie demanded, still not smiling.

"Who do you think you paint like?" Stacey asked.

"Like . . . Corrie Addison," Corrie answered.

Everybody smiled.

"That's the best way for you to paint, or to do anything," said Stacey.

Finally, Corrie smiled.

"May I hang your paintings back up?" Stacey asked.

Corrie nodded.

"Girls, I'm sorry I'm late." Mrs. O'Neal unlocked the door and pushed it open.

"Do you want us to set out paints and clay? Maybe some paper and glue?" Mary Anne asked.

"Are you sure? With all these people around?" asked Mrs. O'Neal, grabbing hold of her pearls.

"It would give the kids a taste of what it will be like to come here. You could even display some of the work they create tonight," said Stacey.

"But, but . . ."

"We'll watch everyone. Claudia and Kristy are coming too. That'll be plenty of help," put in Abby.

"I'll stand out here and greet everyone," said Mrs. O'Neal, claiming a spot outside the door just as I arrived.

"Claudia, you look fabulous!" Stacey called to me.

"Thanks!" I was wearing a long, full, black skirt with red, orange, pink, yellow, and turquoise flowers embroidered along the hem; a loose pink top; and a necklace I'd made out of papier-mâché beads painted to match the flowers on the skirt. My hair was tucked under a black beret, and I had on beaded earrings.

"Did you remember to bring the face paints?" Stacey asked.

We'd talked about how much the kids liked painting jewelry on themselves earlier and decided to bring some face paints so they could do it safely. I pulled the paints I'd brought from home out of my backpack and looked around for a place to set up.

"Stacey, did you see my picture hanging in the museum?" Jimmy asked when he arrived. "We went to see my great-granny's painting, then we came to see mine."

"I saw it and I liked it," said Stacey. She'd settled Corrie with Claudia to help her with face painting.

"Come here." Jimmy grabbed her hand and pulled her into the hall. "My great-granny has a picture of Goldie in all her paintings, and so I'm going to do that too next time. Look, Dad, this is Stacey."

Stacey turned around, smiling broadly, to greet Mr. Cook. The smile crumpled. "You're . . . I thought you were . . ." It was the deliveryman — at least, she'd thought he was a deliveryman when he'd brought the paintings to the house.

"I'm James Cook, Jimmy's dad."

"But you brought those paintings to the house," said Stacey. "I thought you were Federal Express or UPS or something like that."

Mr. Cook grinned. "Just a good husband," he said. "Rebecca needed some of her paintings to give to a committee reviewing her application for art school."

"What's that about art school?" Ms. Madden joined them.

"Stacey thought I was a delivery service," said Mr. Cook.

"I was hoping you were going to say that an acceptance letter had arrived," Ms. Madden said. "But I guess we better see how the estate sale goes first. If we don't make money it won't matter if I'm accepted or not."

"Well, that's not what we're here to discuss tonight. This is Jimmy's night," said Mr. Cook. He wasn't grinning now.

"Jimmy, maybe you'd like to go into the Kaleidoscope Room and show your mom and dad around," Stacey said, trying to change the subject.

"Dad, you have to see the great paints and easels they have here. I wish we could take some of Great-granny Madden's easels home with us for me and Mom to use," said Jimmy, leading the way. "And there are big brushes and little brushes . . ."

"What kind of paints do they use here?" Ms. Madden asked her son. "Watercolor? Acrylic? Tempera?"

"I think they're school paints," said Jimmy.

Mr. Cook followed his wife and son so slowly that Jimmy had to stop and wait for him to catch up. Stacey said he looked confused as he stared through the open door of the art room. She wondered why, since the Maddens were such an arty family.

"How's the face painting going?" Stacey asked Corrie.

"When I smile, it cracks," she said, turning up the corners of her mouth. "I'm the only one with fancy nails, though. Claudia said the paint won't stick to fingernails."

Lots of kids had shown up and they were all eager to try out the Kaleidoscope Room. Stacey stayed busy hanging pictures in the gallery. She and Abby pulled out the screens they'd found in the art room and arranged them in a zigzag pattern down the middle of the hall.

When the crowds had cleared and Mrs. Addison had picked up Corrie, admiring her paintings and her nails, Stacey collapsed in a chair.

"That was fun," said Abby. "It was great to see so many kids here."

"How many more paintings did you do?" Mary Anne asked.

"Three," replied Abby primly.

"Your work is a lot like Pele's," said Kristy.

"On the soccer field it is," Abby answered with a grin.

"My nails looked so nice when I left the house. But I should have known better than to put the decals on top of old polish," said Stacey, peeling a chipped decal off of her left index finger.

I stood very still. "Let me see that for a minute." I grabbed Stacey's hand and studied her nail.

"Tell me, O Powerful One, what do you see in my future?" Stacey asked, and the rest of my friends giggled.

"You have on a coat of polish, then a decal . . ."

"I have on a base coat, two coats of polish, an overcoat, then the decal," Stacey corrected me.

"It's as if you painted over the polish with the decal," I said.

"Sort of," said Stacey.

"So when it chips, you see what's underneath it."

"Plain, old, pink, chipped polish," Stacey said.

"That's why the paint flakes off the paintings in Grandmother Madden's studio," I exclaimed. "Why didn't I think of that before? She wouldn't get rid of the canvases, but she might use them for something else."

"What are you talking about?" Abby asked.

"The painting that I found, the one I thought

was a Madden? Well, the paint chipped off when it fell over," I explained, my thoughts tumbling out as fast as I could put them into words. "It's the right size and everything. Then, there's the Japanese portrait that Jimmy knocked over. The paint chipped off of it too. But wait a minute, it's too big."

"I'm still not sure what you're talking about," said Mary Anne.

"I don't think Rebecca Madden hid the paintings. I think Grandmother Madden herself did! She let her students paint over her pictures. There might be eight or ten of them in the studio. And the portrait could even be a Madden — it could be two of them! Since it's framed, the backing would hide any signs that it was two canvas frames joined together, and the paint is so thick that it would hide the seams on the front. Remember, I told you that her paintings fit together to form bigger pictures? I need to measure it to know if something might be underneath."

"You mean — you found the lost Madden paintings?" Stacey said.

"Maybe. We'll know more when I have the chance to check this idea out."

"Charlie could drive by the Maddens' on our way home," said Kristy.

Charlie was waiting for us by the time the room was clean.

Kristy gave him directions and he pulled up beside the house.

"It's dark," said Stacey. "Ms. Madden and Mr. Cook must not be back yet."

"But I know where the key is," I said.

Everyone piled out of the car. I picked up every loose stone in the walk. "It's not here." I stomped my foot. They must have taken the key with them. "I want to see those pictures."

"They'll still be there in the morning." Stacey put her arm around me.

"But how am I going to be able to sleep?" I'd been so sure that there were Maddens, and now that I had something concrete to investigate I couldn't get inside to check my theory. And it wasn't just curiosity that made me so anxious. I was afraid that if I'd figured it out, someone else might have figured it out too.

CHAPTER 13

"Claudia, is that you? Or do I see an apparition reclining in your chair?"

"Very funny, Dad," I said, not in the mood for jokes so early in the morning. It was Saturday, and I was out of bed way earlier than I would be even on a school day. I hadn't slept very well either. One minute I was sure the small square canvases in the Madden house had original Grandmother Maddens underneath the student pictures, and the next I was wondering how I could have come up with such an idea. I'd know soon, as soon as I got inside that house.

Not many people were outside so early. It was a beautiful fall day, perfect for an estate sale. As I walked to the Maddens', I wondered if people were lined up outside the house already.

As it turned out, a few people were wandering around in front of the house, so I went to the side door and knocked. No one answered.

Making sure that no one was watching, I lifted the stone where Ms. Madden usually hid the key, hoping she'd put it back when she'd come home the night before. I couldn't imagine where they'd gone already.

The key was there. I took it out and quickly unlocked the door, slipping inside and making sure the door shut behind me.

The studio doors were open wide. The Japanese portrait was the first thing I saw. I looked around for the maybe-Madden, but I didn't see it anyplace. In fact, only a few paintings were in sight. I wondered where Ms. Madden had put the others. She'd said she was going to offer them in the sale.

I'd stuck a tape measure in my backpack. Now I pulled it out and held it against the frame of the portrait — ten inches across the top and twenty inches tall. It could be two Maddens together. I felt a rush of excitement. If I could only uncover the cat now. I'd noticed that it was usually in a corner. If I could just take some of the paint off, very carefully, I'd know. I had a strong feeling I should wait for Ms. Madden, but I wasn't sure anyone would believe me without proof. I decided to look for the other canvases first.

I opened the door to the small alcove Jimmy

had shown me earlier. The shock of excitement I'd felt then was nothing compared to the flash I had when I saw what was inside now. A stack of square canvases, all the same size, was waiting for me. I pulled them out. On top of the pile was a plain white piece of paper with HOLD written across it in red letters. I looked at each painting and still didn't see the maybe-Madden. I did know that Ms. Madden shouldn't sell these until she heard what I had to say. I turned around and picked up the Japanese portrait.

"I know your secret now," I whispered to her. "Thank you for finally telling me what you've known for such a long time."

A coughing noise made me look up. I gasped. A woman stood a few feet away from me. It took me about two seconds to figure out that she was the woman who had come to the house for a preview a few days earlier, and who I'd seen at the museum with Dale Ogura. "You scared me," I said. "I'm sorry, but the sale doesn't begin until ten. How did you get in here?" I had to give the woman points for persistence. This was the second time she'd tried to sneak in early.

"I knocked on the door — it was open. I came to pay for my purchases, and it seems you have them right here. Thank you very much." She picked up as many of the ten x ten

137

canvases as she could hold. "I may not have to share these after all."

I started to move slowly toward the door. I did *not* want this woman to leave with those paintings. Besides, something about her wasn't right. There was a wild gleam in her eyes when she looked at the paintings, and it scared me a little. "I'm not sure what you're talking about. Maybe you need to see Ms. Madden."

"Ms. Madden? I *am* Ms. Madden, and these paintings are mine! Rebecca has the house. It isn't fair for her to have these too."

"Who are you?" I asked. She must be crazy, I thought. Calling herself Ms. Madden. Did she like Grandmother Madden's work so much she wanted to *be* her?

The woman laughed. "I'm Suzanne Madden, Rebecca's cousin. I'd like to thank you for finding these for me." She turned and started to leave.

Goldie limped into the room, meowing loudly. She wrapped herself around Suzanne's ankles, making it impossible for her to move. "Goldie! You little devil, there you are." She freed one hand, leaving the paintings wobbling dangerously, and patted the cat on the head. "This cat is the one thing I got from my grandmother's house. I 'adopted' her when Granny died. Of course, no one knows that I'm the one who 'adopted' her, but I love the little dickens. I brought her along when I came to town earlier this week, and she bolted out of the car."

I wondered if she was telling me that she catnapped Goldie when her grandmother died. Ms. Madden — Rebecca, that is — seemed to think her aunt had the cat.

"I'm so glad to see you, little punkin," she cooed to the cat. "I thought I'd lost you."

"Let me help you with those paintings." I reached out to take a few off the top, but Suzanne pulled away. One painting started to fall, but a hand reached out and caught it.

"Hi, Suzanne," I heard Dale Ogura say. "I thought you might try something like this. I guess I made it here just in time. Those are my paintings. Rebecca's holding them for me."

"These paintings belong to *Rebecca*," I said. What was he doing here? Where were Ms. Madden and Mr. Cook? I thought about screaming.

"Don't you dare." Dale Ogura grabbed me.

The next thing I knew, he and Suzanne were stuffing me into the storage area behind the wall.

As soon as Mr. Ogura took his hand away from my mouth to shove me inside, I squawked. They slammed the door shut.

I beat against the door for a few minutes.

Finally I gave up and leaned against the wall.

All I can say about the storage area is that it was dark.

And there was no way out.

CHAPTER 14

I had to think. Someone was bound to come in sooner or later. I didn't want the later to be too late — after Mr. Ogura and Suzanne got away with the paintings. Here I was, locked in a small, dark room, with who knows what (I couldn't even think about what might be crawling toward me), and a little piece of me was happy because I had been right. Grandmother Madden had not destroyed her paintings.

I heard a noise: a rustling, then a clump. Hoping that it came from outside the closet, I pressed my ear against the wall. I heard heavy footsteps, like a man's. I wanted to call for help but waited a minute to make sure it wasn't Dale Ogura coming back for something else. I didn't think he'd hurt me, but I didn't want to take any chances.

"Hey, Dad, the line goes all the way around the house now," I heard Jimmy say.

I knocked on the door. "Jimmy, it's me, Claudia!" I yelled.

Nothing. I knocked again. "I'm in the closet behind the wall. Please, let me out!"

The door opened and I tumbled out, landing at Mr. Cook's feet.

"What on earth?" he said. As he stared at me, he ran his fingers through his hair, making it stand straight up.

"Quick! Did you see Mr. Ogura or Ms. Madden's cousin anyplace?"

Ms. Madden hurried into the room. "My cousin? Which cousin?" she asked.

"Suzanne. She said her name was Suzanne," I said quickly. "The cat was hers. It got out one day when she was snooping around trying to find your grandmother's paintings, then she couldn't find it — "

"Someone took Goldie?" Jimmy interrupted. "Where is she?"

"I *guess* they took her," I said, "but they also took the paintings. All the square paintings, because they were your grandmother's!"

"No they weren't, Claudia," said Ms. Madden, shaking her head. "I know they were the right shape. But they weren't anything like the way Granny painted."

"Underneath. She let her students paint over her work. I *knew* she wouldn't be able to destroy it," I said.

142

Everyone gasped. Ms. Madden's hand flew to her mouth. "But I promised those paintings to a young man, an art student."

"Was he Asian-American?" I asked.

Ms. Madden nodded. "He offered me a very good price."

"It was Dale Ogura," I said.

"Mr. Ogura is an old man," Ms. Madden said, looking bewildered.

"This is his son," I explained.

"Granny's paintings. They *were* here. And now they're gone!" Ms. Madden turned to her husband and he pulled her close.

"Goldie. I want Goldie." Tears streamed down Jimmy's face.

"But wait a minute," I said. "I wasn't in there too long — "

"They locked you in that closet! I can't believe they would do something like that," said Ms. Madden.

"They have to divide the paintings between them and they have to do it someplace. I wonder . . . " I racked my brain trying to think where they might go. I had no idea where Mr. Ogura lived, although I knew where he worked. "I wonder if Estates Unlimited is open on Saturday," I said. If it were, they wouldn't go there because someone might see them.

"The office is closed because the staff is busy working estate sales today. I have a beeper number if you think we need to call," said Ms. Madden.

"The office is closed?" Then it would be a perfect place for Suzanne and Mr. Ogura to run to. No one would question them carrying a pile of paintings into the office. "We need to call the police and tell them what happened. Your cousin and Mr. Ogura may have gone to Mr. Ogura's office."

Mr. Cook and Ms. Madden were out of the room before I finished. I followed them to the phone in the upstairs hallway. Mr. Cook explained what had happened and asked the police to send a car to Dale Ogura's home and one to the office.

Jimmy kept pulling on his dad's shirt. "Don't forget they stole Goldie. Please tell them to bring my cat back."

"They'll send someone right away," Mr. Cook said, hanging up the phone.

"I want to go there myself," said Ms. Madden, echoing my feelings.

"The sale is going to start in about thirty minutes," Mr. Cook reminded her.

"But you could stay here and take care of everything. We'll drive to the office and see what's going on — see if the police caught them," said Ms. Madden.

"Me too," said Jimmy.

"No, you stay here with your daddy. Okay?" Ms. Madden said. "Claudia, you want to come along?" She looked at me. "They'll need someone to identify the paintings, and you need to tell the police what happened to you."

"Okay," I said.

Mr. Cook held out the keys and Ms. Madden grabbed them. We raced outside.

Her car was parked on the street, and we had to push through a throng of people to reach it. If the number of people waiting was any indication, Ms. Madden's sale was going to be a big success.

Ms. Madden drove quickly through town. The police were already at the Estates Unlimited office, standing beside Mr. Ogura's red Mercedes, when we arrived.

"I'm Rebecca Madden. My husband called about some paintings that are missing from our house," she said as she climbed out of the car.

"There's no one here, ma'am. No one at the house either," the officer greeted us.

Ms. Madden threw up her hands. "Where could they have gone so quickly?"

I peeked inside the car. I saw a brochure with Japanese writing on it lying on the passenger seat. "Mr. Ogura had a ticket from Japan Airlines," I said. "I saw it one day last week. Maybe he — "

"Could you call the airport police and have them check on any flights to Japan?" Ms. Madden asked the officer.

He got on his radio and talked for a long while.

"Ma'am, would you and the young lady please follow us to the station? We'll need you to identify the suspects."

Ms. Madden hugged me. I was so relieved and happy that I had to choke back tears.

CHAPTER 15

Jimmy was waiting in the driveway when we finally returned to Grandmother Madden's. People were pouring out of the house, each one with arms full of dishes or clothes or lamps — all kinds of stuff.

"Is Goldie okay? Do you have my cat?" Jimmy asked, running to the car. Ms. Madden took the cat from me and handed her to Jimmy. Jimmy kissed her and hugged her until she me-owed.

"Take her to the tree house and keep her there for awhile," Ms. Madden said. "She might be afraid of all the people."

I climbed out of the car, brushing cat hair off of my overalls. Stacey, Mary Anne, Abby, Kristy, Mallory, and Jessi surrounded us.

"Did the police catch them?"

"Are you all right?"

"Can I see the paintings?"

"What happened?" They all talked at once

and it was hard to make out what anyone was saying.

Mr. Cook joined us. "Come on back to the patio and you can tell us what happened."

"Claudia, you're the one who figured things out. You tell everyone what happened," said Ms. Madden.

I took a deep breath. Everything had happened so quickly.

"Dale Ogura's father and Grandmother Madden were friends years and years ago," I began. "The older Mr. Ogura bought one of Grandmother Madden's paintings, so Dale knew what her work looked like. He also knew how valuable it had become. There's an older brother, I think his name is Dennis, who took lessons from Grandmother Madden, and he told Dale that the students used to paint on old canvases. When none of the Madden paintings turned up after Grandmother Madden's death, Dale figured that Grandmother Madden might have let her students paint on top of her work.

"Stacey, remember when you noticed that Mr. Ogura had paint flakes on his clothes? That was because he was scraping the canvases to see if there was anything underneath. By that time Suzanne, Ms. Madden's cousin, had showed up and called him. She remembered him from the summers she and her cousins spent here."

"I still don't know how I managed never to meet him," Rebecca put in. "You said he was around the house, but I never saw him. Whenever you said 'Mr. Ogura', I always assumed you meant his dad."

"Oh, Mr. Ogura was very careful about timing his visits here. If you saw him, it would have ruined his plan. But he did want to get into the house. He used his job at Estates Unlimited and his father's name to do that — though as we know, he didn't go so far as to take his father's key to Grandmother Madden's house.

"Suzanne and Dale decided to team up and see if they could find the paintings together, since neither one of them was having any luck alone. When Suzanne couldn't get inside and Dale couldn't check all the canvases soon enough, they decided that he would offer to buy most of the old paintings." I paused again.

"I thought I was lucky that someone was going to take them off my hands," said Rebecca, laughing. "He offered much more than I'd thought I could sell them for."

"This morning, Suzanne tried to double-cross Dale by picking up the canvases first. She was surprised to find the door unlocked. I forgot to lock it behind me when I came this morning to check the Japanese portrait. Sorry." I looked at Ms. Madden and she smiled.

"James and I had to run separate errands and we still have only one key. That's why it was under the stone," Ms. Madden explained.

I took another deep breath and continued my story. "Suzanne had gotten to the paintings, but Dale showed up, demanding his share. When I said neither one of them should take the paintings, they locked me in the closet."

My friends gasped.

"It wasn't too bad," I said. "While I was in the closet, I concentrated on figuring out where Mr. Ogura and Suzanne might go next. They had to divide the paintings. By the time Mr. Cook and Jimmy let me out, I'd decided that Estates Unlimited would be the best place for that — if no one was there on Saturday. But when they weren't there I felt as if we'd reached a dead end."

I paused for a second and then continued.

"I looked inside Mr. Ogura's car, and, luckily, he doesn't clean it out very well. There was a travel brochure on Japan lying inside. Seeing it reminded me that Mr. Ogura had had an airline ticket with him one day. On the chance that it might be for today, I told the police about it. They stopped Mr. Ogura at the airport, and he told them the name of the motel where Suzanne was staying. That's where they found the rest of the pictures — and Goldie."

"Hooray for Claudia 'Nancy Drew' Kishi!" cried Stacey.

"I thought you'd found one of Rebecca's grandmother's paintings earlier in the week," Mr. Cook said.

I nodded, remembering the maybe-Madden. "I thought it was a Grandmother Madden too, sort of. There were similarities, but there were also some differences." I still wanted to see that painting again.

Ms. Madden laughed. "You found a Madden all right, but it was a Rebecca Madden."

"You painted that scene?" I said, surprised.

"I didn't know it at the time, either," said Mr. Cook. "I tried to find it in the catalog of your grandmother's paintings."

"That's where it went!" said Ms. Madden. "I've been looking all over the house for that catalog."

We had been too, I thought.

"When I couldn't match it, I took the painting to Mr. Ogura — old Mr. Ogura — and asked him to look at it. I knew that if it was your grandmother's, we'd have enough money for art school for you," said Mr. Cook.

"I don't know how either of you could have thought my grandmother painted that painting. I painted it, thinking it would please her, but she said, 'No, no, no, Rebecca. This is the way *I* paint. You paint your own way.' I probably shouldn't even think about going to art school. I won't be accepted. I was late getting my paintings to the committee to review."

"Is that who you were talking to about delivering paintings?" I asked.

Ms. Madden nodded. "Then I picked up a painting from home and decided I wanted another one. James brought it to me."

"And I thought he was a deliveryman," said Stacey, her cheeks growing pink.

"Anyway, they probably won't even consider my application," Ms. Madden finished.

"Well, I was saving this for when the sale was over and we knew how much money we'd made, but — you were accepted. The call came yesterday," said Mr. Cook, beaming at his wife.

"Is that why you were so cranky about the subject last night?" Ms. Madden asked.

He grinned. "I was saving it for a surprise. I knew we wouldn't have time to enjoy the news or celebrate until the sale was over. But really, what made me cranky last night was all that art stuff at the museum. Even my son knows more about it than I do." Mr. Cook shook his head. "I have a lot of learning to do to keep up with you two."

"I'll be your private tutor," said Ms. Madden, tucking her arm in his.

"I'd already decided that you were going to go to art school no matter what. I'd raise the money some way. You should have heard what Mr. Ogura — old Mr. Ogura — had to say about your painting. He said it was 'masterful,' among other compliments and superlatives. Then the committee said a lot of the same things. We'll find the money somehow."

I laughed. "You don't have to worry about money now. Those paintings are worth a fortune!"

"They are, you know," Ms. Madden said to Mr. Cook. "And I do want to use some of the money for school, but I want to divide it with some of my cousins. Granny didn't know how much her paintings would be worth when she left everything to me. She would have divided things more fairly if she'd known."

Mr. Cook kissed his wife on the top of her head. "You're a very generous woman. Let's go see if there's anything left in the house."

They walked off, arm in arm.

"You're amazing!" said Kristy.

"I would have been so scared," said Mary Anne.

"I didn't believe there were any paintings," said Abby with a shrug. "I guess I'll have to start trusting your Nancy Drew nose."

I brushed off their praise. Now that we'd solved the mystery, I started thinking about the primitive painting I'd begun last week. I had the urge to finish it.

"When will the rest of us get to see the masterpieces?" Stacey asked.

For a minute I thought Stacey meant *my* painting. Then I realized she meant the Maddens. "The police have the paintings now," I said. "After they return them to Ms. Madden, she'll have to send them someplace to be restored. Remember, there's a painting over each one of Grandmother Madden's works. I hope they will be exhibited after they're restored. Maybe at the Stoneybrook Museum." I could already see it, including the three generations of cat pictures — Grandmother Madden's, Ms. Madden's, and Jimmy's.

"Hey, Mallory! Can your brother come over and play in the tree house with me?" Jimmy ran to us, carrying Goldie.

"I'll call and see," she answered.

I decided I'd include Jimmy and Goldie in my painting when I finally got around to it. I was sure Grandmother Madden would like that.

Ann M. Martin

About the Author

ANN MATTHEWS MARTIN was born on August 12, 1955. She grew up in Princeton, NJ, with her parents and her younger sister, Jane.

Although Ann used to be a teacher and then an editor of children's books, she's now a full-time writer. She gets the ideas for her books from many different places. Some are based on personal experiences. Others are based on childhood memories and feelings. Many are written about contemporary problems or events.

All of Ann's characters, even the members of the Baby-sitters Club, are made up. (So is Stoneybrook.) But many of her characters are based on real people. Sometimes Ann names her characters after people she knows; other times she chooses names she likes.

In addition to the Baby-sitters Club books, Ann Martin has written many other books for children. Her favorite is *Ten Kids, No Pets* because she loves big families and she loves animals. Her favorite Baby-sitters Club book is *Kristy's Big Day*. (By the way, Kristy is her favorite baby-sitter!)

Ann M. Martin now lives in New York with her cats, Gussie and Woody. Her hobbies are reading, sewing, and needlework — especially making clothes for children.

THE BABY-SITTERS CLUB

Look for Mystery #33

STACEY AND THE STOLEN HEARTS

Pete Black stood up. "Stacey, I have to go," he said. "There are only a few minutes left. Can you handle things here?"

Rosie had finally finished. I looked around and saw that the hall was almost empty; the buses must have left, and most kids had headed home. "Sure," I said. "I have a few valentine-grams to write anyway." I'd just realized that I'd forgotten to send valentine-grams to my BSC friends. Pete took off and I started writing.

I was just finishing the last one when something made me look up. There was Robert, standing right in front of me. I pushed the final valentine-gram into the bag. "Hi," I said.

"Hi," said Robert. He had a serious look on his face. Finally, the moment arrived. School was over, and the building was nearly empty — except for the two of us. It was time to talk.

"Hey, am I too late?" asked Austin Bentley, appearing suddenly at the front of the table.

I sighed and held up one finger to Robert. "Just a sec," I mouthed. I turned to help Austin. He wrote out his valentine-gram and paid me. I put away his money and gathered up his valentine-gram plus a few others that had been scattered on the table. Then I looked up to tell Robert I was almost done.

But he was gone.

I sighed. Oh, well. If he didn't want to talk, he didn't want to talk. What could I do?

I went to put those last few valentine-grams into the bag.

But I couldn't.

Because the bag wasn't there.

Read all the books
about **Claudia**
in the Baby-sitters Club series
by Ann M. Martin

Collect them all!

More titles...

❏ MG22873-0	#89	Kristy and the Dirty Diapers	$3.50
❏ MG22874-9	#90	Welcome to the BSC, Abby	$3.99
❏ MG22875-1	#91	Claudia and the First Thanksgiving	$3.50
❏ MG22876-5	#92	Mallory's Christmas Wish	$3.50
❏ MG22877-3	#93	Mary Anne and the Memory Garden	$3.99
❏ MG22878-1	#94	Stacey McGill, Super Sitter	$3.99
❏ MG22879-X	#95	Kristy + Bart = ?	$3.99
❏ MG22880-3	#96	Abby's Lucky Thirteen	$3.99
❏ MG22881-1	#97	Claudia and the World's Cutest Baby	$3.99
❏ MG22882-X	#98	Dawn and Too Many Sitters	$3.99
❏ MG69205-4	#99	Stacey's Broken Heart	$3.99
❏ MG69206-2	#100	Kristy's Worst Idea	$3.99
❏ MG69207-0	#101	Claudia Kishi, Middle School Dropout	$3.99
❏ MG69208-9	#102	Mary Anne and the Little Princess	$3.99
❏ MG69209-7	#103	Happy Holidays, Jessi	$3.99
❏ MG69210-0	#104	Abby's Twin	$3.99
❏ MG69211-9	#105	Stacey the Math Whiz	$3.99
❏ MG69212-7	#106	Claudia, Queen of the Seventh Grade	$3.99
❏ MG69213-5	#107	Mind Your Own Business, Kristy!	$3.99
❏ MG69214-3	#108	Don't Give Up, Mallory	$3.99
❏ MG69215-1	#109	Mary Anne to the Rescue	$3.99
❏ MG05988-2	#110	Abby the Bad Sport	$3.99
❏ MG05989-0	#111	Stacey's Secret Friend	$3.99
❏ MG05990-4	#112	Kristy and the Sister War	$3.99
❏ MG45575-3		Logan's Story Special Edition Readers' Request	$3.25
❏ MG47118-X		Logan Bruno, Boy Baby-sitter	
		Special Edition Readers' Request	$3.50
❏ MG47756-0		Shannon's Story Special Edition	$3.50
❏ MG47686-6		The Baby-sitters Club Guide to Baby-sitting	$3.25
❏ MG47314-X		The Baby-sitters Club Trivia and Puzzle Fun Book	$2.50
❏ MG48400-1		BSC Portrait Collection: Claudia's Book	$3.50
❏ MG22864-1		BSC Portrait Collection: Dawn's Book	$3.50
❏ MG69181-3		BSC Portrait Collection: Kristy's Book	$3.99
❏ MG22865-X		BSC Portrait Collection: Mary Anne's Book	$3.99
❏ MG48399-4		BSC Portrait Collection: Stacey's Book	$3.50
❏ MG69182-1		BSC Portrait Collection: Abby's Book	$3.99
❏ MG92713-2		The Complete Guide to The Baby-sitters Club	$4.95
❏ MG47151-1		The Baby-sitters Club Chain Letter	$14.95
❏ MG48295-5		The Baby-sitters Club Secret Santa	$14.95
❏ MG45074-3		The Baby-sitters Club Notebook	$2.50
❏ MG44783-1		The Baby-sitters Club Postcard Book	$4.95

Available wherever you buy books...or use this order form.
Scholastic Inc., P.O. Box 7502, Jefferson City, MO 65102

Please send me the books I have checked above. I am enclosing $_____
(please add $2.00 to cover shipping and handling). Send check or money order–
no cash or C.O.D.s please.

Name_____Birthdate_____

Address_____

_

City_____State/Zip_____

BSC5962

by Ann M. Martin

Collect and read these exciting BSC Super Specials, Mysteries, and Super Mysteries along with your favorite Baby-sitters Club books!

BSC Super Specials

BSC Mysteries

More titles ➡

The Baby-sitters Club books continued...